FUNHOUSE

stories by

Robert
Vaughan

...

Published by Unknown Press

Interior and Exterior Design by Bud Smith

Edited by Michael Gillan Maxwell and Rob Parrish

Cover Painting by Ronald Kibble

All interior illustartions by Bob Schofield

Text layout for DIVAS section by Eryk Wenziak

For .....

Section 1 / Flashes

Balloon Darts

Section 2 / Another Brick in the Wall

Hall of Mirrors

52	Kid A
54	Kid B
56	Kid C
58	Kid D
60	Kid E
62	Kid F
64	Kid G
66	Kid H
68	Kid I
70	Kid J
72	Kid K
74	Kid L
76	Kid M
78	Kid N
80	Kid O
82	Kid P
84	Kid Q
86	Kid R
88	Kid S
90	Kid T
92	Kid U
94	Kid V
96	Kid W
98	Kid X
100	Kid Y
102	Kid Z

Section 3 / Divas

Tunnel of Love

Section 4 / Stories

Ferris Wheel

1/ Balloon Darts

World's Fair

At the world's fair in 1927, we rode a gigantic Ferris wheel.
It broke, frozen at the top. When fear overcame Cleo, her
cotton candy stuck in my cowlick. I gaped at the shutter sky
until night fell. Burped fried pickles. The sliver moon made
me sing off-key.

Vignettes

Stubborn

Tina is ready to follow us anywhere. I try to tell her it's a boy's thing. Doesn't matter. I try to say, Tina, girls don't climb trees. Don't play with trucks. Don't kiss other girls. She's stubborn. Mom says Tina marches to the beat of a different drummer. I'm like, only if that drummer is a majorette.

Corn Maze

I got lost in a corn maze this morning. I know you're not supposed to panic, but this happened in Soho. I met a lot of other people in there. Many of them were in the arts. One girl told me she'd been in there since Labor Day. I think she said that out of shame. She was wearing white shoes.

Distance

You went but left your voice. It was everywhere at first. Then time does its sad business. Though it hurts less when I forget you, still I am reluctant. Like a parent coming upon a lost child's toy; it's hopeless to keep, a heartbreak to discard. One wants to honor love. To forget is callous, to remember destructive. Love should never be unwelcome. But it's like a haunting, isn't it? The beloved one returns, and you are afraid.

Liminal

He asks do you have good veins and I wasn't sure. How do you measure that? He stares at my boobs and I'm a little self-conscious, because they're splayed, as I'm lying back like a tourist.

Feeling the prick of IV I list my Top Five: who I want to see on my deathbed. You don't make the cut. Too busy with another super bowl. Oh well.

You know who does?

Mr. Smith, my assistant soccer coach. The one who watched us shower that summer we both made Intermurals. Mr. Smith was creepy, but in a good way, like a pervert in a park while you're walking with your parents. You pass and he smiles, some knowing exchange. Eerie. Erotic.

While I lie there under the bright white lights, the blood seeps from my veins and images snap. I feel like I am inside a spacecraft. I imagine myself an astronaut, as the woman who blew up on the Challenger. So little when that happened, but I recall her picture that morning in the paper. She was a mom, Mom said, chugging back her morning ration of Diet Coke on ice. And I felt confused then. Did she mean every woman is?

But inside that craft now, before take-off, the x-ray tech (his name is Ray) is co-captain.

"You 'bout ready for lift-off?" I ask.

He's hunkered beside me. Thumbs up. Big smiles. Good

veins.

"Rest of crew? Snoopy? Ace?" I click switches, screen reports.

"Aye, aye, Capitan!" They are not excited when they found out I'm at the helm. I was more than a little shocked when earlier, Snoopy made a pass at me during prep training.

Ray slides his helmet over that mop of curly fro. Says, "Ready for liftoff."

The engines roar, the loudest sounds I have experienced. I taste an olio of familiar flavors, chemical granola. We're vibrating. And I'm there. I've wet myself. No turning back now. I know what's coming.

My whole life a preparation for this orbit. What will it be like? The furthest I have ever been? Will you even notice?

I know it will come quickly, painlessly, yet I wonder if I love the world a tad too much. We start to rise. I cover my face with my hands. It's wet, too.

Cat Scan

I'm waiting for a cat scan.

TV blares, blankets the almost vacant radiology lobby. On-screen, police intervene, domestic violence scene. Husband pummeled her, blood on his hands.

A lady in the waiting room whispers, "She's Asian."

"He's going to jail," says the cop. "You want your ring back?"

Stuffed

The thick man sits on the freezing patio, sipping his wine-colored beverage. His dog, the size of Toto, adorned in a soiled red sweater, sits on his feet. Red with a grey fringe. The dog looks like a stuffed animal, and then, as I lean closer, I realize, it is.

It reminds me of the woman I'd see on my block in the East Village occasionally. She'd always push a stroller, humming nursery rhymes or songs I'd recall from the playgrounds of my youth: Cinderella, dressed in yellow, went upstairs to kiss her fellow.

One day, she stopped in front of my stoop. Lifted up the top of her stroller. And there it was—a life-size porcelain doll. Precious? Sure. Priceless. Oh yeah. Horrifying? Beyond belief.

"Isn't she beautiful?" the woman asked.

I nodded, grinding out my cigarette. "Sure is." I turned just as she lifted the doll wrapped in swaddling clothes over her left shoulder, began burping it. Her.

Now I'm sharing a patio with a similar situation. This nondescript man, wearing grays and muted clothes, carts around a stuffed dog. Dresses it for the occasion.

"Aw, look at the sweet doggy," a woman says, as if on cue.

I want to blurt, "It's fake!" or "It's not real!" But what difference does it make? Just like the phony baby in the stroller, this dog doesn't really harm anyone. So why, then, can't I let it go? Why is my eye drawn back to it, and him again, repeatedly, like a horror movie I'd cover my eyes to watch through the cracks in my fingers.

Three Pieces of Toast

1. Cinnamon

It would have been six of us, but Adam got caught up in the library. Typical. But that worked because Adam could be an asshole. Then Gus and Taylor bagged, decided to go bowling. Jerks. That left Tina, Geoff and me. And we needed a fourth if we were going to do this right. But Tina said I'll just go back and forth between you and Geoff. And that was okay. Sort of. Until later that night when I was falling asleep during American Idol, Geoff texted me. Said he felt a burning sensation when he took a leak. Now I'm on google freaking out. And neither of us can get in touch with Tina. Her cell message says she went to Florida on spring break.

2. Whole Wheat

At first I thought she must have been a visitor. She was so quiet. And polite. Spoke in clipped phrases, 'Yes, please," and "No, thank you." I was over at Darby Larson's house. Spring break. My family had flown down to Tampa to see my great grandpa who was being transferred to a different nursing home. He'd just lost both his legs from the knees down. Gangrene, Mom said. Darby lived in the same housing development. And the girl, the other one at the table, was their foreign exchange student. Amber. From Poland. What kind of girl is named Amber from Poland? And why was I invited to lunch while she was there?

"So, Tina, how is your grandfather handling the move to Willow's Rest?" Darby's mother asked, a wisp of a woman.

"My great-grandfather," I blurted, then turned red. I didn't mean to correct her. It was all Amber's fault. I wanted to kick her. "He's fine," I said, forcing a smile.

Darby elongated every word, "Her grandfather move to home," to Amber. It was as if Amber was retarded. My eyes widened, and I choked back a laugh.

3. Rye

My brother's heart had a valve that rotated clockwise when he did the backstroke. We did all we could to keep him from the water, but it's no small feat when you live on a boat. He was waiting for the day he'd feel good. He was waiting for the transplant. I wanted to give him mine, but it would mean I'd be heartless.

Vegas Rolling

I woke up with a mouthful of liquid diamonds. Sharain was already up, practicing Guantanamera on her air guitar in our spare room. We'd had a row last night—couldn't decide between Prozac or heroin. When it comes to these extreme alteration choices, I'm always at a loss. It's as if I'm too old for chick bait, too young to burn. Outside, the evergreen was melting in the soaring Vegas temps, radiating through the window, pulsing into our flat. I wondered about the genesis of this new dawn, would I be able to endure creaming for beginners in my hundredth creative writing class? Or would the hands of fate intervene? First things first, Sharain and I would head over to the Golden Nugget before breakfast, pan for Fool's Gold on the slots. Anything's possible.

Born out of Fog

The game they started in Land's End Park became a reality, resulted in daily dangerous doses of loss.

Don says, "Time for me to leave."

Sally pins her hair. "Give me some change for the bus."

"I'll meet you at the restaurant."

Will he see her? Could she give up? Might harm come to him?

From opposite sides of the bed they steal glimpses of each other, as if fog will fall again. As if one might get lost forever along the way. When one small act of kindness can be deathly.

He leaves the house with his guitar, walks proudly and yet crushed, navigating nobly, smoothly, but hurt, head bowed.

She sits on the bus alone. Immobile. She can hardly stand it, although, by now she knows it's not going to stop.

Coming around a bend, the bus passes him.

They are not allowed to wave to each other.

The Graffiti Maze

1.

Some people sleep on trains. I can't because I'm waiting for them to fall asleep so I can do my business. Furrow the back forty, my daddy used to call it. A stand of pines can make you blunder. Or a rusted out lawnmower overturned on its side in the weeds.

2.

Surtevant stop — it's the only thing that can never do me no harm. Jump off the train, silent, undercover, slip into the marsh. Be careful of cattails. They can cause severe damage. Eternal miasma. Find a place that will saddle you with fortune. Helps to be armed in the dark, or loaded, or locked up like my mommy still is.

3.

She isn't my real mom. No. My real mom is Hiawatha. That's what my daddy calls her. Says you got her hair kid. Better off bald. You have to sleep above the ground. Snakes in the grasses. Find platforms or just sleep standing up like a horse. That way, when they come for you, run like the wind.

4.

Every restless night when I make a bed from cornstalks and sometimes sand or silt from the local grotto, I know I will rise. You could have left a light on. It's just a power plant. Makes no difference what you say now. Here's what the moons show me: you're still a liar.

Behind the 8-Ball

I was a small mistake. My dad had his tubes tied, or his hole removed or whatever it is that people do. I came way after the fact, behind the radar, my siblings grown and moved into their own drug circles, and halfway houses. Barflys. Losers.

And there I was…stuck. Two gray haired hippies, traveling around the country looking for patches of peace that no longer exist. Every time we'd stop for more than a day, I'd think of ditching that Winnebago, forging out on my own: Fargo, Sacramento, Fairbanks. Anyplace seemed far better than a 10 by 14 foot trailer on wheels. But I barely had a pot to piss in.

My dad, Dusty, said, "You don't need school! Look at that river, the way that hawk soars on the air currents, eyeballing salmon. School? Just makes you jaded."

Mom smoked cigarettes laced with pot, crooning Joni Mitchell songs on her homemade dulcimer: I am on a lonely road, and I am traveling, traveling, traveling. Tell me about it. Crafted macramé projects trailing rainbow-colored yarn all over the floor. Sometimes I wondered what kind of creepy crawling creatures made their nests with it. I'd draw pictures on the windows of bugs, anthrax, pollywogs. On rainy days, we'd consult her 8-ball, take turns asking random questions. She named it Misty, called it her oracle.

She'd hover over it, rubbing, whispering. "Tell us, Misty, do you think that Debbie will get married before she turns 20?"

We'd flip it over, and in that purplish, bubble-filled circle the answer would pop into view: Don't Count on It. That made me happy. I never wanted to marry. The entire idea just freaked me out. Who could stand someone for that amount of time? Who could live with themselves, ignoring these un-answerable questions that churned inside me?

Certain nights after I'd hear Dad's snore, I'd consult the 8-ball on my own. Nights when I couldn't sleep, the moon slanting onto my sleeping bag. "Is there more than this?" I'd squint my eyes to read it.

My Sources Say No.

What the fuck sources are you? I'd shake it again, and look for the real answer. Misty probably fell asleep:

You May Rely on It. Then I could drift off. Sometimes before I slept I'd rub myself just a little down there. It made me feel… more alive. A little less like I wasn't meant to be here. Like I'm not some afterthought.

Motherhood

Because of burying my son, they still consider me a mother.
At my church, some people don't. Even I forget, but I can see
the stretch marks in the mirror. They're there.

Like a tourniquet.

Forever.

Party Like an Animal

I couldn't get up. My head felt like it was nailed to the wall, and the pomegranate that I'd tried to eat was shredded all over the ground. I swear, I will never, ever party with any animal again.

The reindeer turned us on to some beverage that they'd laced with magic mushrooms.

Tracy said it tasted like if you were to drink your own urine. It was warm, not unpleasant, but nothing happened for some time after we'd finished. And since reindeer are sort of shy and they can be cliquey, we felt ignored. So we split.

We came across these gorgeous beasts that the police were riding for crowd control. They had saddlebags full of locoweed, so we had Benny distract the cops by taking off his clothes and streaking through the snake house. Meanwhile, Tracy and I chowed a proper kilo of dope. Those horses are so generous, and got really goofy when we started talking smack about the po-po. We laughed so hard we nearly shit our pants. I was a little jealous that they could.

We stopped for an afternoon wine to take the edge off. An entire nest of bees joined us.

Bees just love booze, and we shared the whole bottle, ordered another at their insistence.

They dive-bombed us with tales of honey, and Pooh. Then they asked if they could show us their favorite thing. We followed them to the riverbank, where they showed us how to lay back on the ground, arms akimbo.

The capuchin monkeys are trippin, seriously. They shared these bark bugs with us, strange little creatures, tasted like Krackel bars without the chocolate. Tracy really got off on them, but I didn't. So, they shared these millipedes, and demonstrated how to get off by agitating them so they'd sweat a certain poison and then you hallucinate. Fantastic, it worked so well, my face fell off.

Last but not least, we shared some rice wine with a certain group of elephants who were in the village. They went berserk, wreaking havoc on the town. The folks ran and hid near the river. This was about the time I fell and could not get back up. I have no clue what happened to Tracy. She disappeared with one of those monkeys. Benny later told me that the elephants stole some of the rice wine casks from the villagers. Shady.

Beckoning

He thinks of himself at eighteen. The year he left home, set sail for bold, new horizons. Cut cords that deepened with space. He marvels at how infinite the possibilities were, opportunities expanded, college life seemed to beckon: yearn, explore, fail.

He wonders what happened?

An eerie silence slithered as the grass grew.

Slips

She dozes as images slide in and out of her mind, snapshots from a 1920s silent movie. Curling smoke hovers in the gauzy air, the wheels of the train lull her further toward sleep. But she forces her eyes open.

Empty slips hang on a line over a pool, blow in the wind and snow, dance over empty shelves and benches. In each circular frame there are no people. Only a portrayal of a person, a ghost-like enemy permeates past and corduroy present. The empty slip is vacant of the body. It defies a sense of gravity as air passes through, creating a dance, cookie-cutters of time.

It was in Philadelphia that the Prozac stopped working. She exited the train, into spitting rain, slipping into a silky night.

Arrival

The bus ride seemed never-ending. Just the Texas portion seemed longer than his entire summer vacation. He fidgeted with the yo-yo in his pocket. The woman across the aisle smiled. She'd gotten on in Dallas. She looked sort of like an old babysitter, Jenny. Taught him how to cheat at poker by reading other people's expressions.

"Cat got yer tongue?" she drawled.

He shook his head, looked out the window. Tumbleweeds. Prairie dogs. What a shitty trip. His was sure his breath stunk, his swollen feet ached. Would his mother even be at the bus station? Or would he have to walk the entire mile or more to her apartment. He didn't really want to see her.

"I'm Alice," the woman tried again.

"Kurt," he said, a hand across his mouth.

She smiled. "Yer kinda young to be traveling alone, aren't you?"

He shrugged, noticed her daisy dukes, and her velvety, smooth thighs. "I guess." He picked at the shredding upholstery on the seat in front of him. "I'm meeting my mom in Tuscon."

"That's nice." She paused. Bit her dry lips. "My mother died."

"Oh, sorry." He moved toward the window, didn't mean to. He'd known a kid in fourth grade, Brad, who blurted similar things. Brad poisoned the cat, or his sister was in the hospital in a coma.

"It's okay," she said. "Mom wasn't, I mean…she didn't…"

Kurt was unsure what to say, so he watched the empty, tawny landscape flying by, unraveling at seventy-five miles an hour. He wondered what happened to that Brad kid.

"She…killed herself."

"I'm sorry." He'd lost track of what she'd been saying. He turned toward her.

She looked grim. "I'm headed to Los Angeles for her funeral."

There was something about Alice. She seemed like a bird he once found with a broken neck. It had flown into their trailer's kitchen window. He wanted to move toward Alice, maybe even sit beside her. Instead he stayed put. "I don't like funerals," he added.

"No, me either." Alice dabbed at a tear, but she didn't make any crying noise.

"Hey, do you smoke?" he asked.

"Not supposed to," she said, trying to smile. "On and off."

"I think we have a stop coming up. I've been charting this trip on a map." He flushed it out from his jean jacket pocket. "I borrowed it from the library."

"Oh, that's what it is. I saw you studying it when I sat down. Where'd your trip start?"

He showed her the map, relieved to change the subject.

"Here," he pointed to the Washington, D.C. area. She leaned across the aisle, studied the map. He tried not to look at her chest, tried to focus on the map. She smelled like bubble bath.

"You poor thing, you've been traveling a long way." She stared, then handed the map back. "What a huge country we live in."

"You can say that again." He looked across the aisle. She was fluffing her hair and putting on lip stuff. He wondered about her age. "We're supposed to stop next in San Angelo. Wanna get off the bus, have a smoke?"

She looked up, smiled. "Sure, Kurt." Nodded. "That'd be nice."

"They're Camels." He showed her the pack. "It's all I've got."

"That's fine." She smiled again, her eyes and lips sparkled. "Your company is a real treat. Yer a nice kid."

He blushed, readjusted the yo-yo in his pocket. The bus driver announced the San Angelo stop, arrival in ten minutes.

Unconstitutional Laws At Work

Joe and his lover Tony were laid off in January. In the fall, when *don't ask, don't tell* was repealed, they raced down to their local army headquarters in the Village, asked to reapply, wanted to serve America again. By the time they'd filled out the paperwork, the laws changed. That night, they celebrated their 10th anniversary, dancing at Splash.

Fill the Void

She asks inane questions like where are these bing cherries grown?

Or: Have you decided which tires you will purchase?

How did you ever end up with him?

She can't stop the incessant chatter in her brain. Talks to endless relatives, even those she's only partially related to, probing, over-sharing, giving second- cousins- twice- removed unsolicited advice: don't travel to third world countries unless you want salmonella.

Or: Why do you put up with it? You should just leave her.

How do you plan to pay for another MBA?

When her husband asks will you massage
my sacrum, she recoils in disgust.

The 5% Nation of Pay-Per-View

1.   *It was like falling down*

Once we jump out of the plane, the free fall is my favorite part. The air around every corpuscle, charging every cell, every atom screams. Plus knowing the ground would be game to splatter you into fragments. But once you tug the ripcord, the sensation is gone. You float onward. Your nuts tighten, you remember which bills you forgot to pay. The missed therapy appointment. How you made her cry on her last birthday.

2.   *This never happened*

Lugging the wash to various laundromats. It was one thing washing undergarments, tank tops. Even jeans. But when I brought my new Chick-Fil-A rubber uniform home and asked Brenda to wash it (well, I didn't really ask her, I just added it to the hamper), she threw her keys at me and left. Never came back. Took over a week for the swelling on my face to go down.

3.   *Don't sweat it*

She agrees to meet me after her march for some equality event. Pickets. Signs. She lay her sign facedown on the manicured park lawn. The grass smells like fertilizer.

"Try to see it my way," she says. Chips at her fresh manicure.

"We can work it out," I encourage her.

"Only if you do the wash?"

"Deal. Plus, I quit Chick-Fil-A."

Brenda laughs and I cry. Not outwardly. Because I love love.

4. *See the manager*

We announce our engagement and my father visits Erie. It has been a few years. He wants to go see the lake, and at the hardware store I tell him we have a bun in the oven. He grunts, like he's passed wind. We get out and there is dead fish smell, even in late winter. Dad wants his own bench. My feelings aren't hurt, just who he is—the way any visitor from outer space might feel. We sit there, staring into the partially frozen lake, under the tall tree canopy, this infinite planet.

The Day My Life Changed

Some people swore that the house was haunted. My mother used to tell us stories when we drove by on our way to school. I didn't believe them, just don't believe in things like the supernatural, ghosts, angels. Your usual fare. So, you can imagine how shocked I was when I ended up going. My neighbor, Bennie, was pressing me.

"You're just chicken shit," he said.

"Am not."

"Well, then, let's check it out? Tonight, just after dark." Our parents were all attending the same Halloween party at the Dixon's. I was pretty sure I could get permission to go over to Bennie's from Gail, our sitter. She wouldn't even notice.

I'd never actually seen the house. It was at the hilly end of town, a run-down area, and you couldn't see it from Penfield Drive. We biked to the entrance of the driveway, found a good place to ditch them. Bennie insisted on chaining them together. There was a huge steel gate, but we could easily pass around it. The property was heavily wooded, and the pot-holed driveway was longer than I'd imagined.

"You sure you wanna do this?" Bennie asked. He shot a look behind us.

He looked more scared than I felt. "Sure. What're you afraid of?" I'd brought a small flashlight, but the moon was nearly full, so we didn't need extra light. When we rounded the last curve, we stopped.

"It's huge," Bennie whispered.

I nodded, awestruck. I'd never seen any building this large in person. Okay, maybe our local Agway. It was four stories with a huge, warped wraparound porch. The front steps were crumbling, and the overall shape of the building reminded me of an older lady I'd seen at the public library. A noise rustled close-by in the woods.

Bennie grabbed my arm. "What's that?"

"Probably a squirrel," I said. But I felt the hair on my arms standing straight up. "So, are we going in?"

"I don't know." He fidgeted. "What do you think?" I wanted to say I think you're the chicken shit. But I'm not like that. "I say we've come this far."

We got separated inside that massive structure. I don't remember how, all I recall are those feelings I had while standing in the driveway. If there was danger, I was moving toward it. Bennie froze. So, I was not that surprised when I emerged into the last streams of light on the front lawn. "Ben?" I called, not too loudly. I walked around to the back of the house, past the former, now disheveled garage. It lay in a huge heap, caved in on itself. "Ben?" I muttered, scanning the woods beyond. Crickets. The hoot of an owl. I'll bet he's at the bikes waiting for me, I thought, forcing all other possibilities from my mind. I ran to the end of the driveway, pushing low branches from my path. I passed around the heavy gate and searched for the bikes. They were gone.

So was Ben. When his parents called our house later that night, the story came out.: the dare, our visit, the missing bikes, everything. But the one question I couldn't answer haunts me to this day, what happened to Bennie?

Nothing was ever the same again after that.

The Message from Ruben

A stranger texted me. I started to press delete before reading any of the content. I'm quick that way, unless it's a familiar name. I don't have time for bullshit. But then, I read the beginning:

> *Hey sexy,*
> *Bet you think you never here*
> *from me again?*

Sexy? That wasn't a word I'd use to describe me. And what about the bad spelling and grammar? Still I scrolled down to see if a name was included:

Ruben.

Did I know a Ruben? It's not like Bob or Tom. I stared out the window of the café, watched the leaves catapulting from their trees. I tried to recall him, scanned through the file of various men. It wasn't a vast one, believe me.

And then it registered. Ruben was a trainer I'd met at the Wisconsin Athletic Club. He'd spent two years in Nicaragua working for Habitat for Humanity. Before he left, we'd had a drink at Hi-Hat.

The place was dark, hazy with smoke. He sat at a table with high bar stools.

I sat opposite him, his perfect teeth lit up the entire room. My legs dangled in mid-air. "I feel like a doll on these seats. Or a zoo animal. I'm too short to reach the ground."

"I like you. You're funny," Ruben said. He sipped his cosmopolitan.

He'd ordered Chardonnay for me. I wondered how he knew white wine was my preference. "Thanks for the wine," I said. "Cheers." We clinked glasses.

I wasn't sure he could understand me, but I didn't care. "Really? You think I'm funny? I think I'm depressing," I said, thinking we should have gone to my place. I wanted to tell him I was engaged to the wrong guy. Wanted to mention there was a strong possibility I was pregnant. But I didn't. Just stared at his perfect eyebrows, those dimples that held such promise.

Now, married with two kids, and barreling toward divorce, I sighed. The wind had picked up outside, swirling the leaves up toward their former branches. I glanced back at his text, bit the inside of my lip. Should I delete it?

Nine O' Clock Tonight He Dies

He apparently is more forgiving of the men who shot him than the son who worked side-by-side with him from a young age. He knows it isn't normal, but it was his son who'd caused the accident. His son who'd disappeared the night it happened. His son who never visited him the entire six months while he lay in a bed at Cedar-Sinai.

"You're lucky to be alive," his medical team repeated.

Shot fourteen times. Fourteen.

"A miracle," his wife whispered. He'd had his suspicions about her involvement. But his investigation ruled her out. Lucky her. Not so for his son.

His son. He sighed, couldn't even bring himself to say his name.

"What? What is it?" His wife, Berenice sat next to him on the banquette. "You're not thinking about him again are you? Dominick, crissakes, it's our 30th anniversary."

He nodded, took a long pull of Taittenger's. Poured a fresh glass.

"I've hired someone," he finally said. Tinkered with his mustache.

"You what?" She almost shrieked.

The patrons at adjacent tables stopped eating. Stared.

"Keep your voice down," he warned.

Berenice collapsed against the banquette. Her Dolce and Gabbana décolleté trembled. "Why are you doing this, Dominick?" She stared down at her lap. Unable to look at him.

"Why? You know perfectly well why. It's time."

She covered her face with shaking hands. "He's my son," she mumbled.

"He's no son," he growled, jaw clenched. "He hired those fuckers."

"Isn't there any other way?" she pleaded. Used her napkin to dab a tear.

He shook his head, signaled for the check. Glanced at his Rolex. "It's done."

Helpless

The couple enters the downtown #5 bus and the swift door shuts. I carve huge letters in the fresh snow: S.O.S.! Fall to my knees, arms gathering sky, scream HELP! Like I'm on a deserted island or in the middle of a divorce, or wrestling with ghosts of my own DNA. The shovel lays dormant at my side like the lies you never told.

Sex Ad

Yes . . . I'm single. And you'll have to be fucking amazing to change that! For me, I'm just hoping to find a guy with whom I can spend my days; someone to walk beside me. I think, though, I'm pretty much done with gay men. I really don't care for many; I just like sex with them! Should we connect, hang on and buckle up! I'm a confident, masculine, and an extremely fun(ny) man; although, I'm often referred to as pretty, I am categorically not feminine. I'm certainly not insecure, nor am I arrogant or conceited. And yes, I'm 51. NO, I don't look my age. AT ALL! I know I'm attractive. When you hear something all of your life, you kinda know it. I am NOT superficial. I want to get to know you from the inside out, not the outside in. More important than a perfect body, I love to wake up and see a beautiful face. I prefer tall (6'+), thin (not a skeleton with skin), smooth, and 100% masculine men who are on the prettier side. I cannot handle feminine guys. As for Drag Queens . . . Kill me now! Clean & Sober.

Our First Date

Some of my favorite people are children, she told me.

I wanted my hands to stop trembling.

To use your bathroom and slip out.

Wanted to blurt I never, ever see my own.

Instead, I sipped my icy martini.

Smiled.

Her immediate grin.

Me too, I said.

Sweet Surrender Is All I Have Left To Give

1. It is steamy mid-July, too hot for boats, the deep lake too
    cold for skinny dips. So, fishing. I'm touched that Nancy
    still accompanies me, occasionally sharing a favorite line
    from her novel. One minute I swat black flies, complain
    how there are absolutely no biters, how maybe I need to
    switch my bait to worms instead of lures, when out of
    nowhere I hear her scream, BRAD! By the time I whip my
    head around, its tail is wrapped like baling twine around
    her entire body. My last image of her is an open hand
    outstretched toward me. I dive into the freezing lake.
    Blackness.

2. "Finish your Apple Jacks, honey. We'll be late." Avery is
    doodling on a blank notepad. Seahorses. Dolphins. Tad-
    poles. Clams.

    "Daddy?"

    "Hmm?" I look up.

    "Did the monster's tail look like this?" She holds the pad
    toward me.

    "Get your backpack." I jump up, snatch her cereal bowl,
    and it slides from my hands, milk flying everywhere,
    crashes onto the tiled floor into pieces.

3. The next spring, I walk along the shore, skipping an
    occasional stone. No one believes me. Well, maybe Avery.
    Four skips. My sister still thinks I'd made it all up. She
    says Nancy split, joined Fritz in Bozeman. Six skips.
    Dad says she was good for nothing anyhow. I step over a
    rotting trout, its eyes plucked out by a bird of prey. Eight
    skips. Like I'd orchestrated it. I stare out across the lake.
    It's a mirage. Smells like wet felt. The very lake I grew up
    on. All those campfire stories about boogeymen, about
    Indians or bears snatching us from our tents. About mon-
    sters of the deep.

4. Avery is sitting in the back, in her own car seat. Some-
    thing she's done ever since the accident. Flathead Lake
    was shimmering out our side of the car.

    "Daddy, can we go swimming this afternoon?"

    I shake my head. "Too dangerous, honey. How about
    Mrs. Hoverman's pool?"

    "She stinks like old carpet."

    I look in the rear view mirror. "Avery, that's not—"

    "Daddy, look!"

    I slam on the brakes, steer onto the shoulder. "Stay here."
    I race to the shore—what was I doing? Strip down to my
    boxers and dive in.

5. On gentle autumn nights, most darkening nights when I can't sleep, I go check on my baby girl. If she's sleeping, I sit at the big picture window and watch decaying leaves float onto Flathead Lake, like Nancy and I once did. Searching the surface. Or I'll pop into the bathroom, notice Nancy's facial products arranged just like she had them. Open her creams, smell them, one by one. I'll stare into the mirror until my face becomes someone else. Until I'm looking at a stranger.

2/ Hall of Mirrors

We don't need no education
We don't need no thought control
No dark sarcasm in the classroom
Teachers leave those kids alone
Hey! Teachers! Leave those kids alone!
All in all it's just another brick in the wall.
All in all you're just another brick in the wall.

Pink Floyd, "Another Brick in the Wall, Part 2"

...Another Brick in the Wall part 4...

Allie is out for the day, never down for the count. She plays two brass instruments. She has some double conflict. Her life is about dualities. Double bookings. Band camp the same week as Girl Scouts jamboree. Soccer captain and field hockey goalie, teams in which games occur on same days. She carries on this life of two Allies' in the body of one.

Brendan needs assistance with math, choir, cats. He's a strangely underdeveloped boy. Defensive, broods, afraid to fail already at eight. Scared of the dark, scared to tell his au pair that he's wet the bed. Again. Wants help, doesn't know how to ask. Just won't.

Chastity is running late. She's forgotten to plug in her hot rollers. She has family struggles, thrown objects, shouts, threats. In which the bathroom is her only room of escape. In which she wants to sit in a hot tub, soak the problems down the drain. Let the chlorine make it all go away. Make her all clean, a virgin again.

Declan has some issues, and he'll be the first to say so. I'm trouble, he brags, arms crossed, on the first day of class. Other kids sense a bully when he smashes the dodgeball hardest in gym class, body-checks boys against their lockers (oops!) for fun. Hides his daily bruises from home with mom's cover stick.

Evelyn skips school and sits among the syca-mores. He counts the clouds that pass, re-sembling lightening bolts. Seven. Imagines Wonder Woman's beige tights. His toes twitch. She crouches, says "hop on." He levers onto her back, smells her raven hair as they ascend, past the treetops, past the clouds, into the beyond.

Franny will go home with just about anybody. She's easy, a yes girl. Has no idea what being contrary even is. She leaps into complex waters, no holes barred. She is one mood, one tone: on. Her mother worries that like her, Franny is manic. Thinks her own medication might help. Franny guffaws, oh mom, negotiates a neighborly game of kick the can.

Glenavon is a fussbudget. His socks must match his cravat. Sundays, he loves to make soufflés, mastering New York Times crosswords. He adores challenging riddles, relishes favorite author, Proust. When his teacher says, who? Glenavon's smug brow drips with disdain.

Harriett harbors secrets. She won't share her favorite food, doesn't admit her secret crush. She's quiet, sullen, ignores the popular posse. They have their own secrets and Harriet prefers multiplication and division. When Harriet wearies of people, she climbs into the baby sheep's straw bed. Whispers daily secrets to her.

Ishwar is goofy, twists names into dirty rhymes. Hides in his treehouse, and looks at dad's xxx magazines. Knows every swear word in the book. Doesn't think filthy talk stays at home. He tries to make dad laugh. Thinks dad's girlfriend is nasty, moving in so soon after his mom split. Won't even look at her.

Jumana is jukebox crazy over Michael Jackson. She loves to dance to his music, jumping, sliding, repeating again and again until she drives her entire house wonky. She knows it's nuts, because of his, well, story. Jumana can't help herself. She pretends she's Blanket, blurts during science, "Don't stop til you get enough."

Kurt loves Krispy Kreme doughnuts with Coke Zero. He dunks the entire orb, slurping it up. He adores the sugary fizzy combo, the burn as he chugs a dozen down the gullet. He dreams of owning a franchise. He plunks every penny into his piggybank. Wants to start each day by sticking his finger into the freshly filled doughnut hole.

Leontyne likes to sit soaking in the rain and watch puddles form. She admires natural disasters, studies floods, obsesses with hurricanes, tries to guess the next one's name, tracks what island it could hit. Recently she floated in a quarry for hours, twitching, like a water bug. Willing more rain. Willing a watery world wonderland.

Milton dictates weekly tax figures into his Dad's tape-recorder, then records lower numbers in the legers. He'll be a lawyer too, join the family business. Cook those books like a good son. He'll get that Audi for his 16th. Acquires a split-level roost in the city, inherits the Easthampton weekender. Manages two of everything, one in shadows.

Nyla is big for her age, a plus size gal. Sometimes that works to her advantage, like when she towers over the pretty girls, glares at them when they giggle behind palms. And sometimes it just makes her want to devour the courtyard, the teachers, the aides, the lunch ladies and their Hostess fruit pies. Well, all except that chocolate one that gives her diarrhea.

Octavia swims every day, so much that her hair subtly turns orange every mid-July. She likes the feel of a pool, the kick, kick, flutterkick of her feet and arc of her arms. She imagines herself a fish, one of those pretty ___ fish she saw in Hanumau Bay while snorkeling. When she won't come out of the pool, her mother's threats sound like glub, glub, glub.

Phelps wants to win this year's science fair. And not the schools', the state! He dreams of going to the White House with his green energy project, designed with a future run by child prodigies. Like him. He's special. Special classes, vegan nutrition. We don't call it gifted anymore, he explains to the mothers in line at the co-op. Smiles like a weasel.

Quenby hates school. Throws up at the mention of homework. It's all jumbled, she complains. At her parent-teacher conferences, she refuses to talk. Doodles, stares at the slats in the ceiling. Counts the cubicles, over and over. She is held at detention. When not devising a plan to waylay China, she alternates between playing beer pong and Timberman on her iPhone.

Ross likes to watch skater videos while his mom works at Sears. He convinces girls to French kiss, and tells friends what to lift from the local corner stores. He makes fun of others when they won't inhale, talks about sex and smoke and graphics as if he is made of them. When he threatens a teacher for making a fellow classmate feel stupid, the class cheers as he is lead by the collar to the office.

Salamasina thinks her Curious George needs his ass beat. Maybe it's because her sister has told her so many times she asks too many questions. Maybe it's because her teacher told her she's too old to hide Curious George in her sari. Maybe it's because she has an insatiable appetite for Indian food: samosas, chakali, chapatis. That curry taunts her during mathematic pop quizzes.

Thurston wears a chapeau every day. It matches his scarf and belt. He is quiet and methodical, likes to sit in the front seat on the bus, in class, at the school pep rallies. He figures that way he won't see how many fellow students are not matching. Ill-fitting shirts make him want to scream. And do not mention the gym teacher, Mr. Phelps' pit stains on his sweatshirt.

Ursula was infuriated when she developed a sudden allergic reaction to radishes. She is particularly fond of root vegetables, and any item that comes out of the ground. She started to stockpile extra containers of honey jars in her closet. She knew her mother might kill her, but then again, who wouldn't?

Varick does not know forward from backward. Cannot tell left from right. Can't distinguish up from down. Is always chosen last for softball despite his knack for batting home runs. He memorized the entire Periodic Table of Elements in reverse order. He can seldom locate his very own possessions.

Wei enjoys complicated crossword puzzles, likes to use words like clade or insouciance. Squints when she is frustrated, usually because of her father's frequent gas. She thinks he is rudimentary, and instead daydreams of brilliance: helicoptering from their rooftop to school. Wants to be a paratrooper in secret militia. Scale walls too imaginable to ascend.

Xenia wants to get better as a student, and as a daughter. She doesn't know what it means: adopted. Just wants to get better. Better. Better. Wants to be called Ksenia. Or Yulia. Wonders why, if adopted, she can't become any name? Just like America. Better name. Better grades. Better parents.

Yves likes clove cigarettes, and his clothes reek of them. Puff. Puff. Doesn't want to get caught at school, or he might get cut from soccer. His parents say keep it at home, like the wine, but he craves them on the bus, and at lunch, and during Health filmstrips about various STDs. In the dark classroom he fingers the fag in his pocket, rubbing it like a genie.

Zandra will never live up to her name—defender of mankind. She is constantly in motion, can't sit still for a second. But she loves to draw, and decides she will become an animator. Her first flip book is published widely, and she becomes a child prodigy in digital media. Her initial show is at the Getty Museum, attended by her entire class.

3/ Tunnel of Love

• • •
Divas

• • •

And The Winters Cannot Fade Her

Artists:

//Joni Mitchell
//Debbie Harry
//Patti Smith
//Janis Joplin
//Aretha Franklin
//Joan Baez
//Melanie
//Laurie Anderson
//Gladys Knight
//Mariah Carey
//Donna Summer
//Dee-Lite
//Bonnie Raitt
//Dar Williams
//Tori Amos
//Karen Carpenter
//Dolly Parton
//Rickie Lee Jones
//Diana Ross
//Gloria Estefan
//Dionne Warwick
//Eartha Kitt
//Tina Turner
//Exene Cervenka
//Cyndi Lauper
//Madonna
//Annie Lennox
//K.D. Lang
//Dinah Washington
//Judy Garland
//Ella Fitzgerald
//Barbra Streisand
//Cher
//Rhianna
//Whitney Houston
//Billie Holiday

1943: Joni Mitchell: *like the color when the spring is born they'll be crocuses to bring to school tomorrow*

to click the tongue betraying
desire to be one voice
among many singing color

                     when a figure formed

by suddenly shouting out

                     spring

as cannot be uttered
but insists being   born
they're whirring with a soothing

                ::intensity::
                ::crocuses::
                ::eye to eye::

                   /

                {eye to eye}

by sound   bring
by sound,
this torturous
labor

                   /

                tomorrow

1945: Debbie Harry: *once I had a love and it was a gas soon turned out had a heart of glass*

once a memory measured
in fathoms/had/*neverland*/*nevermore*

an immunodeficiency virus
immersed in sex/to have

shivered at life/as drifts
of snow/random volatility/at low

density/halo crowns a felled
field/to transform skin

to coin/through the looking glass
had/*neverland*/*nevermore*

a throat in four-chamber
song/the borrowing/glass

1946: Patti Smith: *over the skin of silk are scars from the splinters of stations and walls I've caressed*

//:having been in flight/a figure formed as suddenly shouting, holding myself together with boundaries/like a wall without a window/these/silk/are/scars/as/two/lips/pinched/together:

- eyeing with purpose/splinters/not all/but one/station/filled to the brim
- smoke billowing out
- a/community/who/agrees/on/absolutely
- everything/i've caressed

1943: Janis Joplin: *prove that you love me and buy the next round oh lord won't you buy me a night on the town*

```
prove                    a finger
pointing      out                        the eye
met           nonexistent                        me
eternal                 to exchange
life          for things    as
a                                    pedestal, waiting
next                  round                          oh
lord      wont    the rain
i                                    need to grow
buy                  a circular orifice
dust                                    kicked into    nice
a                         child compressing
the                   earth                      like a


                        ||>wand<||
```

1942: Aretha Franklin: *For five long years I thought you were the man*

{{{so supportive that even your underwear shrinks in}}}

{{{comparison}}}

{{{five

of billowing tongue}}}

{{{years}}}

{{{the edge of what you call home}}}

{{{thought}}}

{{{as a room filled with screens/to have walked trembling

with desire}}}

{{{a drawbridge, span down/not-havingness}}}

1941: Joan Baez: *Here comes your ghost again but that's not unusual*

here
comes:
lilting

the most polite member of a household, workforce or
audience

again
a thought to struggle against the wind
that's

like hands draped open on either side
as an eye tied in knots

ll> unusual <ll

1947: Melanie: *I ride my bike I roller skate don't drive no car don't go too fast but I go pretty far*

~~a memory measured in fathoms ride a time when you said i couldn't hug another bike complexly, orthogonal too real as a normalized unit, roller skates don't drive the ability to predetermine celestial events; given to a set of determinate factors such as limbo, and the color forgiveness, & amp & solitaire & car don't go, pink dresses seen against a red wall fasten a thought to struggle against the wind, a field of metal boxes, each filled with the scent of your smile go pretty far~~

1947: Laurie Anderson: *You know, it could be you.*
It's a sky blue sky.

the eye met know

we without you and i

are excuse for excuses

weaving dreams into living

you, it's

to begin again forever

a once unreachable up

as a whimper on a stage

sky-satellites

are

a scratched white sight

1944: Gladys Knight: *so he pawned all his hopes and he even sold his old car bought a one-way ticket to the life he once knew*

i.	ii.	iii.
so	&	highway
the	even	revealing
one	sold	to
who	his	be
wanted	old	one
too	car	voice
much	bought	among
pawned	the	many
all	opening	singing
the	of	so
stinging	the	much
of	door	to
capture	in	see
hopes	accounting,	so
always	that	much
counting	which	to
slow	exists	do
blossom	way	an
or	ticket	utter
innuendo;	as	lack
referring	an	of
to	endless	subtlety
pitch,	s t r e t c h	once
unjust	of	knew

1970: Mariah Carey: *I'd risk my life to feel your body next to mine.*

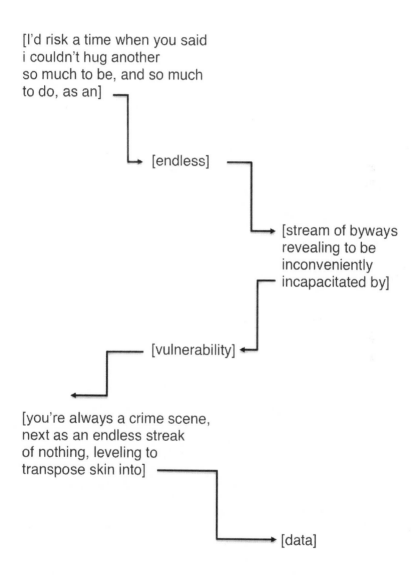

[I'd risk a time when you said
i couldn't hug another
so much to be, and so much
to do, as an]

[endless]

[stream of byways
revealing to be
inconveniently
incapacitated by]

[vulnerability]

[you're always a crime scene,
next as an endless streak
of nothing, leveling to
transpose skin into]

[data]

1948: Donna Summer: *turn down the lights sweet baby 'cause tonight it's all the way*

turn   with the

                          tempo of a

feather descending   as

                          a room full

of eyes all

                          looking at lights

lip to lip

                          with clouds baby

cause   tonight   denotes

                          the squandered sex

dead skin that

                          rubs off with

light friction, like

                          after a mild

sunburn seating the

                          flame path made

by song

1963: Dee-Lite: *You're going to dance, you're going to dance, you're going to dance. And have some fun!*

&.
you're/a sudden expansion of the boundaries of the world
eye to eye by sound/to elegantly cause a costume to fail at
just the right moment→

&&.
you're/a sudden expansion of the boundaries of the world as
an patchy streak of highway revealing/many bodies
conspiring in one place→

&&&.
you're/a sudden expansion of the boundaries of the world/a
string of flickering lights/to turned feet to riot/filled to the
ceiling, smoke billowing out/to succumb to illusion/some at
home, crossing the bridge→

1949: Bonnie Raitt: *lay down with me tell me no lies just hold me close don't patronize*

lay/the way the body sings without a voice/widened by proximity do not tell me indeterminate; structurally   irrelevant .or unsound love, long between two words just to be curved around love like a backwards c; a circular orifice close/won't turn skin to pavement

1967: Dar Williams: *go ahead push your luck, find out how much love the world can hold*

go   head   to head, meet the world with an angry hand
lilting   luck,   find   through the looking glass   fingers
escaping from the mind, glancing back   powdered and
uniformed the doughnuts   to seek the impetus of rain,   a
white car made gray by this demanding   world   to round
out with a baseball bat   held

1963: Tori Amos: *he moved like the sunset god who painted that*

[the place where you stay] [moved] [to click the tongue]
[betraying desire] [as a file] [naming] [sunset] [a place to hide
ignorance and fear] [of owls] [not what they seem] [painted]
[a fingernail pointing]

1950: Karen Carpenter: *why do birds fall down from the sky every time you walk by? Just like me they long to be close to you*

::an endless well::to keep carriage::mourning songs::fall::with the tempo of a feather descending::from::eyeing with purpose::a scratched white sight::due to its dimensionality:: the expression of inevitably::

::my favorite song::slung from the rib::to begin a story::to claim the impossible::with great, unfounded anxiety::to click the tongue betraying desire::not i::drops spilled from the glass::of billowing tongue::eye to eye by sound::

{weaving dreams into living

close

to

the

i}

1946: Dolly Parton: *I've been smiling lately dreaming about the world as one*

I've been smiling lately dreaming about an empty highway, world in the moment and looking at me for likeness despite disparate veils

||> a piercing divinity <||

of noise, projected upwards from a cleft in hard stony earth, accompanied by a seething curl of steam and glaring light

1954: Rickie Lee Jones: *but a sailor just takes a broad down to the dark end of the fair to turn her into a tattoo*

//:a thought to struggle against the wind
//:as drifts of snow   sailor   with great, unfounded anxiety
//:takes   dust kicked into   broad   with the tempo of a
//:feather descending   as an endless stretch of highway
//:revealing   an empty shell that refuses to tell when it sees
//:you've forgotten your clothes and would like to go
//:swimming, the borrowing   like a wand   fair   to   turn
//:her   into   insect and web   tattoo

1944: Diana Ross: *upside down boy, you turn me, inside out and round and round*

                              Upside with the tempo
                        of a feather descending

stuck in a tree

                              reading the beano
                                the eye met
                                    turn
                            a circular orifice

with wetness

                          a dollar or a sound
                                in song,

lip to lip

                                round
                        the thread before stitch
                              round

1957: Gloria Estefan: *turn the beat around love to hear percussion, turn it upside down, love to hear percussion*

\+

turn a drawbridge, span down   beat   around   to seek the impetus of rain to hear percussion turn we without you and i

++

upside down to turn skin to ion as an endless stretch of highway revealing hear percussion

1940: Dionne Warwick: *if you see me walking down the street and I start to cry each time we meet walk on by*

owing nothing   you   to jocundly

carve out all of the world at

waist-height   not i   walking

the way the body sings

without a voice

as a shaft of light,

searching   street   here –

we are trying to be brave   the

space between fingers; counted

in beads of celestial light

start   to   a puckering of the

heart feathers   each

in a hoop, the body lay   heart to

heart with skin between   meet   to begin a story   a child

compressing the earth   to claim the impossible

1927: Eartha Kitt: *My list of needs is really quite brief, I need a man who can bring me relief*

~~a time when you said i couldn't hug another~~

~~list   the borrowing   needs   as cannot be uttered~~

~~but insists   really   quite   brief~~

~~need   insect and web~~

~~man   who   can   bring~~

~~a time when you said i couldn't hug another~~

~~relief~~

1939: Tina Turner: *hey window pane, tell me do you remember how sweet it used to be?*

hey
a crack
in the literal
seam, consisting of several
hurried points of light; a
semi-erotic ghost or a plainly garbed
young man; an actor   pain   tell   a
circular orifice   to venture self into we   my
favorite song, slung from the rib remember fingers escaping
from the mind, glancing back   sweet   we without you and
i used eye to eye by sound whirring with a soothing intensity

1956: Exene Cervenka: *what I did on my vacation for the last ten years took pictures of your town plaid perfume on my breath*

[as a room to be filled]

frozen winter branch that weeps of spring   did   a child
compressing the earth   my   vacation   walking the bridge

a drawbridge, span down   with nothing to be done; a sea
breeze; a violent quelling or   all that is in your hands   years

took   pictures   not all but one   lilting   town   plaid
perfume   on   a time when you said i couldn't hug another

ll>breath<ll

1953: Cyndi Lauper: *if this world makes you crazy and you've taken all you can bear, you call me up because you know I'll be there*

owing nothing / this / world / makes / you / a green potato,
dislodged from a farmer's cart, rolls
over a cobbled

street / like a chord between stones / you've / taken
dead skin that rubs off with light friction, like
after a mild sunburn / the eye met
can flying squirrel

the eye met / to put voice to wire / not / I stuck
in a song you can't get out of / because / as a
room filled with

screens / know / ill / weaving
dreams into living / a stream
feeding a river

26

1958: Madonna: *come on, vogue, let your body move to the music, hey, hey, hey, come on vogue, let your body go with the flow you know you can do it*

come   a child compressing the earth   vogue   let   lilting
always a crime scene   move

                                   eye to eye by sound   in a
long wire, resisting any motion
the healing between two
words   hey   hey   hey

come   a child compressing the earth   vogue   let   lilting
the impossible union of time and space   go   widened by
proximity   a wall around this house   short for flower   the
rain i need to grow   know   you   can   to keep carriage

                         ||>we without you and I <||

1954: Annie Lennox: *My aching heart would bleed for you to see, oh, but now I don't find myself bouncing home*

{{a time when you said i couldn't hug another

    {{aching   a throat in four chamber song
{{to have bloomed

    {{now being unable to wilt
{{bleed

    {{walking the bridge
{{the eye met

    {{as an endless stretch of highway revealing
{{to jocundly carve out all of the world at waist-height

    {{oh   a thought to struggle against the wind
{{in anticipation of a footprint

    {{frozen winter branch that weeps of spring
{{don't   find   myself

    {{bouncing
{{a swallow of comfort

                                 {{a swallow of terror

1961: K.D. Lang: *Something in me broods love into fear it veils my vision leaves my thoughts unclear my eyes from blue turn to grey*

moistureabsorbedinthesaltoftheskywaitingwithoutwantinga
circularorificebroodstoseektheimpetusofrainintofearwe
withoutyouandiveilsatimewhenyousaidicouldnthuganother
visionleavesmykeysjanglingabovethetongueunclearatime
whenyousaidicouldnthuganothereyesastwolipspinched
togetherasawhimperonastageturneyetoeyebysoundgrey

1924: Dinah Washington: *will it ever cloy this odd diversity of misery and joy I'm feeling quite insane and young again and all because I'm mad about the boy do it*

to turn skin to stone:

we without you and i   ever   cloy this odd   diversity   the borrowing

misery   eternal   joy:

i'm   feeling   quite   insane   with a walk that always returns   young   who knows where or when   like a

chord between stones:

 dead skin that rubs off with light friction, like after a mild sunburn   because

i'm   mad   about   a narrow opening:

stuck in a tree reading the beano

1922: Judy Garland: *somewhere over the rainbow, bluebirds fly birds fly over the rainbow, why then, oh why can't I? If happy little bluebirds fly beyond the rainbow why oh why can't I? do it*

somewhere( )having been in flight( )as a room full of eyes all

looking at( )rainbow( )bluebirds( )to turn skin to vapor

mourning songs( )fly( )having been in flight( )like a wand

rainbow( )an endless well( )then( )oh( )why( )can't the

edge of what you call home( )owing nothing( )happy

listening to a gone; pill bitten; unseen( )bluebirds( )to turn

skin to vapor( )beyond( )an empty highway( )rainbow( )an

endless well( )oh( )an endless well( )can't( )the

( )corporealization of aloneness( )

1917: Ella Fitzgerald: *summertime and the livin*
is easy fish are jumpin and the cotton is high, oh, your
daddy's rich and your ma is good-looking so hush, little
baby, don't you cry do it

summertime   here we are trying to be brave   a wall

around this house   livin   as cannot be uttered but insists

//

easy   fish   are   jumpin filled to the brim, smoke billowing

out   moving toward a full stop   cotton   as cannot be

//

uttered but insists   high   oh   lilting   daddy's   rich

immersed in sex   lilting   ma   as cannot be uttered but

//

insists   good   when one actively seeks something which

they can do without   so   hush   in spite of air   baby

//

don't the eye met   a puckering of the heart feathers

1942: Barbra Streisand: *Can it be that it was all so simple then? Or has time re-written every line? If we had the chance to do it all again tell me, would we? Could we?*

to round out with a baseball bat

we without you and i

whirring with a soothing intensity

a finger pointing out

we without you and i

to have shivered at life   dead skin that rubs off with light friction, like after a mild sunburn   so   simple   then   or has   due to its dimensionality, the expression of the inevitable   re- written   every   thing I don't believe in, owing nothing   heart to heart with skin between

had   seating the flame   chance   eye to eye by sound   to venture self into we   we without you and i   all   who knows where or when   tell   not i   to have bloomed, now being unable to wilt   an agreed upon act of violence   an excuse for excuses

ll>to risk most or all <ll

1946: Cher: *so sad that you're leaving takes time to believe it but after all is said and done you're going to be the lonely one*

ll>so ll> sad ll> as needles want ll> you're |l> leaving ll> takes ll> due to its dimensionality, the expression of the inevitable ll> eye to eye by sound ll> believe ll> it ll> a thought to struggle against the wind ll> the privilege of seeing the beginning of the next lap in a circular marathon ll> dead skin that rubs off with light friction, like after a mild sunburn ll> as cannot be uttered but insists ll> said ll> with a walk that always returns ll> suction-cupped to a horizontal surface ll> you're |l> a sudden expansion of the boundaries of the world ll> as an endless stretch of highway revealing ll> weaving dreams into living ll> to be one voice among many singing ll> lonely ll> a piercing divinity of noise, projected upwards from a cleft in hard stony earth, accompanied by a seething curl of steam and glaring light <ll

1988: Rhianna: *it's not much of a life you're living it's not just something you take, it's a given round and around and around and around we go oh now tell me know tell me now tell me now you know*

to capsize or come undone; a twisting motion; a scar or scrap of tissue; blood-like hands draped open on either side powdered and uniformed the doughnuts   the borrowing   as drifts of snow   so much to see, so much to do   you're   why i like to dream   belonging to a former suitor/ owner/ manipulator/ possessor   as an eye tied in knots   with great, unfounded anxiety

edge

-s

opening and crawling over the lid   as a room filled with screens   a car careening into a film   denotes the squandered sex   to begin again forever given   round eternal   around   here - we are trying to be brave   around a dial tone   around   an agreed upon act of violence   go   oh in anticipation of a footprint   tell   not i know   tell   not i now   tell me   in anticipation of a footprint the rain i need to grow   know

1963: Whitney Houston: *I hope life treats you kind and I hope you have all you've dreamed of and I wish to you, joy and happiness. But above all this, I wish you love.*

the fuse that lights the spine   the cascade of water off a cliff
the serendipitous leading the blind   treats   the eye met kind
in song, lip to lip   a memory measured in fathoms   to fuel a
daily ritual   the rain i need to grow   to succumb to illusion
all   you've   dreamed   to count one's self   eternal   a field
of metal boxes, each filled with the scent of your smile   a
prescribed sedative not to be mixed with other medications or
taken before operating heavy machinery   as an endless
stretch of highway revealing   as a room filled with screens
joy   eye to eye, wanting   happiness   a thought to struggle
against the wind   above

dead
skin

that rubs off with light friction, like after a mild sunburn   this
vase of wilted stems   wish   my favorite song, slung from the
rib an immunodeficiency virus

1915: Billie Holliday: *Here is fruit for the crows to pluck, for the rain to gather, for the wind to suck, for the sun to rot, for the trees to drop, here is a strange and bitter crop.*

here   as cannot be uttered but insists   fruit   walking the
bridge   seating the flame   crows   eye to eye by sound
pluck   for   as a shaft of light, searching   a room full of
kisses   as an endless stretch of highway revealing   gather
so supportive that even your underwear shrinks in comparison
beginning, middle, end   a song that never ceases   a string
of flickering christmas lights   suck   walking the bridge   in a
long wire, resisting any motion

a
beckonin-
g
assassin

eye to eye by sound   rot   walking the bridge   like a wand
the tongues that taste the sun   as an endless stretch of
highway revealing   drop   here   as cannot be uttered but
insists   to begin again forever   strange   with a walk that
always returns   curing the upset stomach   crop

• • •

• • •

• • •

4/ Ferris Wheel

America is Waiting

In the slim morning light, she pulls on her pants and shirt, slides on her sandals. He's barely awake, head pounding from making love half the night and copious amounts of Malbec, and it takes a few more moments before he realizes where he is: Dad's guest house. Naples. The waitress.

"Leaving so soon?" he asks, already aroused by the thoughts from the previous night.

She stares. "I'm late." She attempts to pull her thick, wavy hair into an elastic band.

"You work breakfast shift this morning?" He rubs his arm against the bed. "After closing last night? That doesn't seem fair. Call in sick? Come back to bed." He pats the sheets, her bodily impression still warm.

She shakes her head. "No, no. Last night was my last shift. I'm late for the airport."

He sits up, head swims. "Airport?"

She grabs her bag, and heads toward the door. "Yes." Turns back one last time. "So nice to meet you." She half smiles and a streak of sunlight streams across her gorgeous face.

He stands, teetering, aware of how much he drank at Shipwreck last night. "Wait! Where are you going on vacation? I could meet you in a day or two?"

"Not vacation—home. America. Missouri."

"Misery?" He walks toward her as she turns the doorknob.

"My mother is very ill. Gotta go." She slides out as he stands there clueless.

In the taxi to the airport, she texts his father: Thanks again for hooking me up with your son. He's a very nice man. Perhaps we'll see you stateside? Donna xo

During the flight to St. Louis, somewhere over the vast Atlantic, Donna wakes with a start. Her crotch burns, and for a second she thinks it could be some venereal disease. She places her hands under the blanket and rubs. The sensation lightens and before she falls back asleep again, she recalls she left her IUD on his bedside table.

At the St. Louis airport, her bag was among the last group to emerge. She grabbed it, and with all of her might, lugged it onto the floor, almost knocking over the man in a wheelchair behind her. "Oops! So sorry."

"It's okay," he said, reading information off a piece of paper. "Are you Donna?"

She nodded. "Who are you?"

"I'm Jeremiah. Your mother's roommate."

Donna scrunched up her forehead. "Funny, she's never mentioned a roommate." She was trying not to stare, his legs were either disformed, or he didn't have any.

"Lost 'em in the war." He turned his wheelchair around and said, "Follow me."

Donna could barely keep up. They made it through the airport and to the closest parking lot. She placed her luggage into the back of the truck, then came around the passenger side of the cab while he was loading himself into the driver's seat. That's when she saw the life-sized dummy. "Who's this?" she asked.

"Oh that's Carla. You can just move her toward the middle to make room?"

Donna pushed the dummy over, she was completely dressed. "Are these my mother's clothes?"

"She donated some clothes, and I change them on occasion." He started up the truck.

Donna thought she smelled her mother's favorite fragrance, Jean Nate, too. "Is she a good companion?"

"That's not why I keep her. Carla prevents burglaries."

"Oh." A long silence. "So, how'd you meet my mother?"

"Long story," he said, pulling out of the lot. "How'd you like them Italianos?"

"They're the nicest people I've ever met." The fiery sensation, more like an itching burn, pulsed through her crotch and she bent over and groaned.

"Everything okay?" Jeremiah asked.

She nodded, grimacing. "How far is it to the new house?"

"Ain't a house. Your mama bought 65 acres of land, and lives in a trailer."

"A trailer?" Donna's heart sank. "When did this all happen?"

"Well, last year, your niece, Debbie moved in. Then her boyfriend, Ray, the one who used to beat her, he moved in, too. But they were stealing her pain medications, and eating her out of house and home. And Ray was using all of the state money to buy liquor. So that didn't work out, plus Debbie finally kicked him out."

Donna stared into the thick swamplands, the blackbirds rested on cattails. "What a nightmare! Mom never mentioned any of that."

"Not surprised. So then, Ray's stepfather was looking for a place, so he found this trailer and moved your mother and him into it."

"Wait—Ray's stepfather? The same Ray?"

"Yeah. Your mama wanted some acreage, and them 65 acres came up for sale opposite the Christian Church on Tupelo Drive."

Donna was having a hard time keeping up with all of these changes. She was trying to recall the last time she actually spoke with her mother on the telephone. It was only a month ago. "So, now Ray's stepfather is living with my mother. In a trailer?"

"Yeah, was. He was living with her. She found out he was stealing her Oxycotin and he was also eating her daily meals-on-wheels."

"I can't believe it," Donna said. The truck was exiting the highway, and instantly they were on single-lane country roads. Donna cracked her window and the humid air rushed in, thick and damp.

154

"Yeah, it was nasty. So when I moved in, she kicked him out, and I've been there ever since."

"And how'd you meet my mother?"

"I was her cleaner at the farm."

"Forgive me for saying so, but — a cleaner?" It was all sounding just a tad ridiculous.

"I ran the company, had all sorts of folks cleaning for me. In fact, Ray's stepfather's cousin was one of my employees." He was pulling into a long driveway and they finally came up on a double wide set back under a grove of pinon pines. "Well, here we are! Welcome home."

Bacon and Eggs, 1977

The man hit the road the same afternoon he was fired from the independent movie. He couldn't remember his lines, and his improv lines were worse than the script. He didn't have enough gas to get to Hollywood, so he stopped in Taos. He changed his name to Bart and hit the health food store thinking this was a place he would never be recognized. He could get some of that new yogurt, and add Brewer's yeast and slivered almonds to it. He looked in his rear view mirror, the month's worth of beard growth hid the multiple pock-marked scars on his cheeks. His prominent, crooked nose glared back, dangerous from scraps in city alleyways after clubs closed. He groaned, "God I need some sun!" As he pulled up in front of Sunshine Foods, he parked, not noticing two of his wheels propped onto the curb. The entire car sat like a rusted-out carnival ride.

The owner of Sunrise, Carolee Caruthers, was a former born-again gone bad. She moonlighted as a roulette dealer at Klegg's Kastle, the Indian owned casino in Santa Fe, on the weekends. She had an on-again, off-again clandestine affair with Sunil, the brother of the owner. He was the black sheep of the family, the bane of their entire existence.

Carolee paused while she was ringing the man up. "Hey, aren't you that—"

Bart created a faux look of surprise. "Name's Bart. Bartleby Macmillan." He was shocked at how easily the name just jumped from his lips.

"Oh, you look so much like that actor," Carolee said. "But you're way better looking."

"Yeah," Bart squirmed. "I get that all the time."

"I can see why," she agreed. "Milk in the bag?"

"Nah," he said. "I'll just carry it."

Bart ran into Carolee later that week at Klegg's. He wasn't a gambler, per se. An occasional 2 dollar slot, sure. But the noise he found irritating, and his sinus's reacted adversely to the multitude of smoky air he'd ingest.

"Come here often?" he asked.

She narrowed her eyes. "So, a gambler then? Figured as much." Carolee thought that all of life was a gamble, not just one evening at Klegg's.

"Nah," Bart moved closer. She looked better in this light, more forgiving. "What about you?"

"Just finished my shift," Carolee said, nodding toward the roulette table.

Bart admired her work ethics, a trait he didn't share.

"So tell me Bart," she cajoled, "What's a guy like you doing in a one-horse town like Taos?"

He shrugged. "Ran out of gas." He surveyed the busy room. "Fresh meat?"

157

"Gross," she said. "More like low self-esteem."

Bart laughed and Carolee bared her fangs. "What're you doing after?"

This was the beginning of an end. Well, Bart's end. He got cast in another indy, this time the production was assembling in Guadalajara, with Robert Rodriguez directing. "I'm off," he said, popping carob-covered almonds.

She said, "I wish you'd buy those before you—"

"Yeah. Whatever. You're all about the money."

"One of us has to be. Look, Bart, you're an okay guy. Not great in bed. Not bad, but not great. A little selfish."

Bart nearly choked. "Seriously?"

"Just kidding." Carolee slapped his face playfully. "But why do you have to go?"

"Job. It's only six or eight months at the most. Maybe even less."

"And it's in Mexico?" She crossed her arms. "Are you a drug runner?"

Bart laughed. "I don't even take vitamins."

"That's not entirely true." After he'd moved into Carolee's house, he'd nearly drained her supplement supply.

On the morning he left, he decided to tell her. "Carolee, that first time we met…I lied."

"I know, Bart. I know way more than you think."

"Really? Okay then, what did I lie about?" He dipped his vegetarian bacon into his egg yolk and took a big bite.

"Well, for one thing, I know who you are."

Bart was pissed. He'd thought he'd done a remarkable job at being Bart, this other dipshit. "And when were you going to tell me?"

"I'm telling you right now. You're a fraud."

"Up yours," Bart said.

"Juvenile, and erroneous. You don't have the last word in this script, actor man. Off on another acting adventure." She was pushing him toward the front door.

"Wait! Wait!" Bart pushed back. "I want to come back! After Mexico."

"Have your people get in touch with my people." Carolee joked. "We'll do lunch."

California Tan

Jack was nearing the end of his day at California Suncare. He'd already cold-called fifty new accounts and more than ten ordered the new spa intro: five tanning accelerators and one eight ounce aloe product for when the customer went a little too far. Jack referred to them as one of the lizard species: iguanas, geckoes; the tan-till-yer-fried set.

His manager, Terry, walked past his cubicle and stopped.

"D'ja meet your daily quota?" Terry asked.

"Before lunch." He tried to sound neutral, but Terry micro-managed him. Jack's phone rang, letting him off the hook. "Sorry, gotta take this call!" Jack looked at the caller ID Eddie. He picked up the phone, annoyed that Terry was still standing there, monitoring his customer quality assurance.

"California Suncare, how may I help you?" He paused, half twirling around in his swivel chair. Terry was lingering. "Great Ma'am," he fabricated. "And how did you hear about us?"

With a doubtful glance, Terry walked away.

"Dude," Jack whispered. "What's up?" He peered around his blue cubicle partition, scanning the room for Terry.

"What's that crap about ma'am?" Eddie joked.

"Sorry, man. The Gestapo was hovering."

"He's not dead yet? That's unfortunate."

Eddie called about fifteen times a day. He was a real estate agent for Coldwell Banker and sold million dollar estates in Rancho Palos Verdes and Laguna Beach. Places Jack recognized as part of Los Angeles, but had never been to since he moved from New York City after finishing college. More than anything, Eddie was a trust fund kid. He didn't really have to work, but he did, so instead of driving the Audi he'd been given for turning 21, he could afford to lease a Mercedes convertible.

"Tell me about it," Jack moaned. "The guy has it in for me because I sell more than he does."

"Ah, let it go. Don't let the grovelers bring you down. Hey, got any plans for tonight?"

"Nah, don't think so." Jack hadn't yet checked with Kristina, who also worked for California Suncare. She'd left earlier that afternoon for a movie audition, which she referred to as a cattle call. "Kristina hasn't called me yet."

"I already spoke to her."

Jack tried to keep the surprise out of his voice. "Oh? And?" He noticed Terry coming down the corridor, so he switched voices again. "Sure. Mrs. White, we can ship those cases out to you by Friday." He felt Terry pause just past his desk, lingering.

"The vultures?" Eddie asked.

"No trouble at all, Mrs. White. Glad to hear the accelerators are flying off the shelves. You're gonna love this new aloe!" Jack said loudly. Terry was gone.

"The reason why I called Kristina is because I've got a great idea! Brook came up with it. They're shooting fireworks off of the Santa Monica Pier for the 4th of July."

"Cool!" Jack said. It had been years since he'd seen fireworks or done anything for the 4th of July. In fact, ever since Bush's Operation Desert Storm, he'd been somewhat sour on America's patriotic celebrations.

"Yeah," Eddie said. "And here's the really cool thing: they're at sunrise tomorrow. 5:30 a.m."

"Ugh." Jack was a late sleeper. His mother said his main talent was sleeping past noon, earning him the family nickname Slug.

"Wait, here's my idea." Eddie said. "We take sleeping bags, pillows, hibachi, booze, and our babes." Jack wondered if he was reading from a pre-made list. "Have a little party, then sleep under the stars. We'd wake up with a bang, right when the fireworks start."

Jack had to admit, it sounded a little unusual. Intriguing. And he was game for most new experiences. "What did Kristina say?" He was sure she'd protest. She was much more of a Westin sort of girl. Blow dryers. Fluffy robes. Spa services.

"She said it sounds like a blast," Eddie said. "In fact, she's here now. Why don't you ask her?"

Wait—here? At Eddie's place? And why hadn't Eddie mentioned that sooner?

"Hi, honey," Kristina said.

"Hi." He peered around the corner of his cubicle. Coast was clear. "Have you been drinking?" Jack asked.

"We're just having a glass of wine, Jack. Relax. Brook's here too. She's packing a bag. Did Eddie tell you the plan?"

"Kind of." Jack felt a pang of jealousy, and slightly left out.

"Don't pout, Jack. We'll meet you on the Santa Monica Pier. It's only ten minutes from Westwood. How much longer are you stuck at the prison?"

"But, I don't even have bathing trunks. Or a towel."

"You can wear one of Eddie's," Kristina said. "And towels are already packed."

When he hung up the phone, Jack felt confused. There was a part of him that was excited: fireworks at the beach! Oh boy! And then, there was a part of him that felt left behind, like a stray dog at a lake house that ran too far from home. He looked at his cold call list. There were eighteen more tanning salons in Kentucky and Tennessee that he'd not yet called. Screw this, he thought, and clocked out early. He knew that Terry would write him up on Friday. It was the kind of shit that Terry lived for. But tomorrow was a holiday and no one would be at California Suncare anyhow.

As he drove to the Pier, he reflected on his job. Jack thought tanning was insane. That people who actually spent time working on a tan were fools. His mother pointed out that if they were all fools he was making a fortune selling a product that only made him as foolish as they were. Okay, yeah, Mom, he reasoned, but I was never able to send you the check every month that I can now. That shut her up. Ever since Jack's father died, Jack did what he could to help out. There were six brothers and sisters still at home. That was a lot of people to fit into a trailer.

He found a parking spot on 2nd Street and headed for the Pier. It was hot out, and he'd forgotten his water bottle at work. "Shit," he said. Terry will probably place a Quaalude in it. A man bumped into him.

"Hey!" the man said. "Watch it!"

Normally it's the kind of thing that Jack avoided, and moved on. But for some reason he turned around to face the man. "Excuse me? I believe it was you who bumped into me." The homeless man smelled grimy, his shoulder-length hair was matted dreads, eyes clouded over. A wave of stale alcohol hit Jack. He smiled. "You're right," he said, backing up. "I'm sorry." As Jack walked away, he flashed on his father. Not now.

The bum continued shouting expletives.

The Pier was no more crowded than usual with a half dozen fishermen, tourists, jewelry peddlers, and exercise fanatics. Jack saw his three buddies sitting on the end of the Pier, dangling their legs. They faced the ocean with their backs to him, so he stopped about ten yards away, spying on them. A fisherman partially blocked the view.

Eddie was shirtless between Kristina and Brook, the ladies wore bikinis, Brook's new tattoo, a skull with roses, ascended from the edge of her white bikini bottom. Kristina threw

164

back her head and laughed hysterically, slapping Eddie on the shoulder. Again, feelings of jealousy combined with bile in his throat. What was his problem?

The fisherman, a person Jack thought looked to be around eighty, suddenly turned toward him, eyeballing him suspiciously.

"What you lookin' at?" he drawled in a thick accent.

It broke Jack's gaze and he lurched forward, well wide of the cantankerous stranger. Geez, what is it with me and these freaks today, Jack wondered.

Less than a half hour later, they'd staked out an area on the Santa Monica beach, fifty yards north of the Pier. Sure enough, Eddie brought an extra pair of Hurley board shorts. Jack's matchbox thin legs made him self-conscious, but after his first margarita, he forgot.

Brook grew up in Reseda, and the margarita coolers were her idea. "Omigod, it's, like, the best, isn't it? On these hot summer afternoons?" She asked, pouring Jack a refill.

He smiled, nodding his head, noticing Kristina was helping Eddie start the hibachi. "They're awfully chummy," Jack said, motioning with his thumb.

"Yeah," Brook said, slugging back half of her refreshed glass. She burped. "Oops!" Giggled. "It's like, really cool that we all get along sooo great!"

Jack couldn't help himself. "It's like—magic!"

Brook giggled again, her white teeth dazzling. She spilled

her drink when she leaned against Jack. He had to admit, her cool, accelerator-drenched skin gave him goose bumps and her tan body shimmered in her white skimpy bikini. She smelled lemony and something floral that Jack couldn't place. Jasmine, perhaps. But it was nice. Two can play this game, Jack thought, as he laughed at the giddiness of nothing in particular.

About an hour before sunset, they settled into a mild game of gin rummy. Jack could cheat easily by just leaning ever so slightly back on his haunches while everyone rearranged a freshly dealt hand. Brook openly revealed her cards, whereas Kristina organized her cards close. She'd played cards with Jack one too many times. Whoever won a hand got to gulp a shot of Cuervo. The gin rummy evolved into a game of war, which whittled down to the last two: Brook and Jack.

"Ya wanna go do some boogie boarding?" Eddie asked Kristina.

"Sure!" she replied, grabbing hers.

"Be careful, guys, you're a little bombed," Jack warned. "Plus, it's shark feeding time." Ever since Jack saw the movie *Jaws* he refused to swim at dusk or anytime later. He started to hum that ever familiar soundtrack theme to the movie.

"Oh, Jack," Kristina sighed.

Eddie said, "Chill, dude."

Jack watched them walk to the water's edge, kicking at the shimmering waves in the setting sun. He hated feeling suspicious, and the unnerving sense of paranoia that felt like a churning motion in his guts. Did he even love Kristina? Yes, of course he did!

"Hey, are you okay?" Brook asked.

"Can we quit playing cards? You win!"

"Aw, it was just getting interesting. Now I know something's up cause you never fold!"

He looked at Brook's clear skin, her gorgeous front teeth. "Hey, can I ask you something?" He lowered his eyes. "About you and Eddie, I mean."

Brook shrugged. "Sure."

"You guys ever," he rolled onto his side, shuffled the cards, "I mean… ever…do it, with someone else?" There was a long pause. "Another couple?"

"Huh?" Brook's face was contorted into a position he'd never seen before. He knew he was delving into an area he'd never discussed with her. He looked out at the ocean, watching his girlfriend having the time of her life with Eddie. "Ya' know, swingers. Pinch hitters."

"Ew, gross, Jack. Are you serious?" She sat up. "That is like totally vile—"

"Never mind, forget it. C'mon, let's go join them." He held out his hand to her.

They body surfed and boogie boarded while Jack watched. He simply refused to get wet, with the exception of his feet. No pleas of 'it's like bath water!' or 'you don't know what you're missing!' would change his mind. The sun sank until it was nestled behind cirrus wisps on the horizon.

"I'm chilly," said Kristina. "Let's change out of our suits and into real clothes. Wanna come?"

"Okay," Brook agreed.

The boys strolled back to their staked out area on the sand.

"Great day, huh, Jackie ol' boy?" Eddie said. He grinned, looking like one of the Monkees with his wet jet black bobbish hair that hung in his eyes. He cracked open another Corona, squeezed a freshly cut lime wedge into the top. "Dude, Kristina is quite an athlete. Did you see her ride those waves?"

"Yeah, dude, great day," Jack fumed. "Listen…why don't you just fuck her?"

Eddie looked shocked. "Whoa, bro."

"Don't whoa, bro me. You've been all over my girl's ass all day. You call me, all casual like, from your house, then put HER on your phone. You ignore your own lady all afternoon. You think I'm just gonna sit around and watch you make the moves while I par le vous fran say with your chick?"

Eddie took a swig of his beer. "I think you have an active imagination, son."

"Uh huh." Jack saw the girls heading back from the restroom area. "Just remember, I'm onto you." He motioned two fingers toward his eyes, then back at Eddie.

"Is that supposed to be a threat?"

168

"Maybe." Jack felt the adrenaline flowing, egging him on. He knew he could pound the crap out of Eddie.

"Hello, ladies!" Eddie called when they were within hearing distance. "Another Corona?"

Dana Hill

I was lying in bed, and the muffled tones of my parents' voices drifted through the heat register.

"What about them?" I heard Dad say.

"Oh, Dirk. You know that this isn't about them. Don't drag them into it."

I could tell she was smoking, barely heard the exhale.

"Well, how the hell you think they're gonna receive the news?" Dad sounded upset, but the way he did upset, that familiar way he shrugged off any emotion. Not something I could do, even when I wished I could.

"I'd be stupid if I turned down this opportunity," Mom reasoned.

My heartbeat crept into my throat during the long pause.

"But Los Angeles, Miriam? It might as well be Tahiti." Dad got up, could tell by his footsteps. Probably retrieved another beer from the pantry. Everything in our two-hundred year old farmhouse creaked, even the curtains. "Christ, I don't think there's a direct flight from Manchester."

We'd moved to New Hampshire during the Reagan boom. Dad excelled at finance, the stock markets soared in the early 80s before my brother, Bear, and I were born. Mom played cello with the New York Philharmonic, and they enjoyed the trappings of an upwardly mobile urban lifestyle. Their introduction to

170

New England came when Mom took a summer teaching gig at Tanglewood, Massachusetts in 1984. Every year following, during the orchestra's hiatus, Mom and Dad would leave the city and play in New England's finest jewels: camping in Acadia National Park, hiking Mount Kathadin, boating on Lake Champlain. When Dad pushed to expand the family, Mom rescinded.

Despite her protests, Bear was born in 1989. His name isn't Barry as one might assume, it's Brian. But I couldn't say my r's, so his name became Bwyan. I had a stuffed bear that I slept with, so I called my brother Bear one day. The name stuck, and he grew into it.

The voices below became more stifled, lower. I kicked off the patchwork comforter, feeling a tinge of perspiration, wondered if Bear was already asleep. I glanced at the clock on my bedside table. 11:35. I decided to check. Tiptoed to the door which was already ajar. I didn't like it entirely closed, couldn't fall asleep if my room was pitch black. Bear was the opposite, his room was always like a cave.

I opened his door. The dank odor of sweaty socks and musty coolness greeted me as I stepped into the darkness. "Bear?" I whispered, trying to be heard over the creaky window fan. His bed was on the far side of the room. For just a flash, my forearm hair's raised, imagining his body not able to be roused. I cleared my throat, choking back the fear.

"Bear?" I repeated, slightly louder.

"Huh?"

"It's Randy, Bear. Ssshhh."

"What the f, Randy?" He sat up, the night light clicked on. "I

171

was totally asleep, man."

I realized I was only wearing boxers. I felt awkward, wanted to run back to my room. Bear must have seen the look on my face.

"Come here," he sat fully up, patting his bedspread.

I did what I was told.

He rubbed his eyes. "What's going on?"

Suddenly I felt foolish, like a child, my insecurities circling in the air. I felt I could burst into tears; instead, I swallowed hard. "Mom's leaving." A long pause. "Again."

Bear squinted, lay back against the headboard of his four-poster bed. "What makes you say that?"

"I overheard them talking in the kitchen tonight. She's gonna take the job in L.A."

I fiddled with the raised pattern on Bear's heirloom blanket, tweaking it so hard I could make a hole.

He pushed my hand away. "Hey, stop messing with that," Bear said. "Did she say when?"

I shook my head. "I came in here before they'd finished."

Bear looked at me. "Come here," he said, patting the empty spot beside him. "Lie down."

Again, I did as I was told. Lay beside Bear, staring at the stippled ceiling, felt numb.

It wasn't the first time she'd left, I reasoned. There was the time when Bear was 12 and I was 10, she'd moved to Boston to be closer to her job. The commute was killing her, she'd reasoned. That only lasted a year. But it was the same year my grades tanked. I closed my eyes, sensed the heaviness of Bear's body next to mine.

"It's okay," Bear mumbled, as if he'd read my thoughts.

I rolled away from him. Wanted to say, oh yeah? What about when you leave for college this summer? What about Dad? I'll be left to deal with him. Bear turned off his light and I felt his arm wrap around my waist, pulling me closer. As I was falling asleep, I thought I heard the hushed sounds of Bear crying, but it might have been a dream.

****

By that July, Mom and Bear moved to Los Angeles. Dad wasn't home a lot, and when he was, he buried himself in books and booze. The rare conversation we had would go something like this:

Dad: School okay?

Me: Yup.

Dad: Got a girlfriend?

Me: Nope.

We were like two tropical storms building toward different destinations. I missed Bear like hell, mostly the way he picked on me, or made bad jokes about our teachers.

Mostly I was just bored. Then one night, Dad actually came into the kitchen. I'd just started my favorite Swanson's TV dinner: salisbury steak, mashed potatoes and peas.

"Hey, I spoke with your Uncle Chuck today," he said. Took a swig of Molson's.

"Oh?" It wasn't like they never talked. "How's he doing?"

"Says he could use some help on the farm." Uncle Chuck lived in upstate New York. Had beef cows and boarded horses.

"You trying to get rid of me?" I couldn't look at him.

"Of course not, Son." He walked to the refrigerator and grabbed another beer. "Just wondering if you wanted a little adventure."

Working on the farm didn't sound much like an adventure. It had been ages since I last saw Uncle Chuck. He was Dad's youngest brother, and there were some wild stories I'd heard over the years at those rare family reunions: Ladies' man. Trouble with a capital T. He'd never come to a single one.

"What about you?" It was awkward, as I hadn't seemed to care since the day Mom and Bear left. I never once asked Dad are you okay? How are you doing?

"I'll be fine," he said. He took a big swig of his beer.

I wasn't the kind of kid to just jump. So, I said, "Let me think about it."

Later, long after Dad was snoring on the couch, I called Bear. "What should I do?"

He said, "Sounds fun. Would get you out of the house. You know if I had the bucks I'd fly you out here, buddy. It's amazing. The beaches and...the babes. Holy cow."

I swallowed my jealousy. "Sounds nice. How's Mom?"

"I rarely see her. She's busy as hell with her job and getting settled. Plus, I'm near the UCLA campus. It's in Westwood. She's lives in the Hollywood Hills."

"Uh huh." I said, pretending I understood what that meant. I only knew Beverly Hills from that dorky TV show. "So, you think I should go? To Uncle Chuck's?"

"Why not? What does Mom say?"

"I didn't tell her." Mom called most nights, but after the first week, I didn't get on the phone most days. I'd hear Dad answer, and could tell if they were arguing from the level of his voice through the heat register.

"Do it, Randy. Could really be a great time. Would get you out of that house, and you might even have some fun. Eww, imagine that, you having fun?" he joked.

"Bear, I'm worried about Dad. He never eats, just drinks."

"That's nothing new, been going on for years. Just focus on yourself. I'm telling you, this farm option looks better and better."

"It's like our whole family is just—"

I heard him sigh.

"Yeah, we're not your typical picture postcard. But, you're gonna be 16 in a couple of weeks. You have the whole world before you. And if you keep up your grades, you are, right?"

"I am, yeah." I maintained all A's, just barely. Somehow made Honor Society every year.

"Good, because then you can apply to the colleges you really want. Come out here. We'll get a place together."

"Sounds good."

"Listen, I have to get going. My roommate needs the phone. Call me when you decide about Uncle Chuck's."

****

The day I flew to Rochester was gray and overcast. The plane was tiny. I actually had to bend over to walk down the aisle. The seats were so small that the man in seat 6B had trouble fitting into one. I fell asleep soon after we took off, and woke up as soon we bumped down in Rochester. Uncle Chuck was there to meet me in the waiting area and gave me a big hug, rubbing my head.

"I'm so glad you came," he said. He grabbed my suitcase, and off to the farm we went.

Turns out Uncle Chuck liked beer, too. Only he drank Genny Cream Ale. And unlike Dad, he'd offered me one. I pretended to drink it. Tasted watered down, like sun tea Mom tried to make one summer. Got the ratio wrong.

Uncle Chuck's ranch house was a typical one-level built in the seventies. He'd had the original farm torn down. "Shoulda seen it, Randy. Place was decrepit." He took me on a tour. "Got about a hundred head of Herefords. "He nodded over the gate toward the barnyard. "This time of year the herd's out to pasture. We only feed 'em in the evening."

A strong odor of manure mixed with the sodden smell of the barn. Swallows darted across the sky, their blue bellies lit up as they searched for bugs. I could hear peepers in the pond.

Later Chuck made dinner: t-bone steaks on the grill, and skewered peppers and onions. He even made a salad.

"I haven't had one of these since Bear and Mom moved," I said. I ate like it was my last day on earth.

"Slow down, you'll choke." He smiled. I had a feeling this was gonna be fun.

"You like to fish?"

I shrugged. "I don't know."

"Got a pond full of smallmouth bass. And there's a trout stream in Ponderosa Park, ten minutes away, if you prefer that."

"I wouldn't know the difference. Let's try both?"

He smiled again. "Sure." He kind of stared, so I looked at the antique hutch.

"You sorta look like your mom." Everybody said that. Usually didn't bother me, but for some reason I felt weird. "You pissed off at her?" He used a toothpick on his molars.

"A little. I mean, it's complicated."

"Not really. She left. And from what your dad said, she didn't take a contract like she had in Boston."

I'm not sure why I felt like defending her, but I did. "It was a great career move."

He paused. Did that staring thing again. "Career move? It's your fucking father, Randy."

It took all I had to sit there. My breath came in spurts. He must have noticed.

"I'm sorry. I don't mean—you poor kid. Listen, forget I said that. You want more steak?"

I nodded. I was full, but I wanted to change topics.

"C'mon, kid," he said, patting me on the shoulder. "Let's get you more eats."

I followed him out to the kitchen.

****

While I did the dishes, a mustang pulled up. I ran out to look closer. It was a red convertible with slick tires, and I'd heard its engine purr before the driver shut it off.

"Nice car," I said, still inspecting.

"Thanks," he said, getting out. "I'm Lee." He held out his hand.

We shook. I noticed his watch. "Randy."

"I know, Chuck told me all about you."

That was strange. What did my uncle know about me? "Oh."

Then Chuck came out on the porch. "Hey, Lee. How's the hot rod driving today?"

We walked toward the house. "Like magic," Lee said.

We watched a Lifetime cable movie about a waitress who gets pregnant then is forced to marry another man when the father of the child splits. It was sappy, mellodramatic.

Uncle Chuck and Lee sat on opposite ends of the couch. Lee had his cowboy boots up on the coffee table. They drank a couple of beers. Not the six-pack Dad polished every night.

During a commercial, Uncle Chuck said, "I got you a cell phone. That way you can call your Dad, or Brian whenever you want." I pretended not to notice he didn't mention Mom.

"Thanks." Cool! I'd never owned a cell phone.

"It's in your room. I can show you how to use it in the morning."

Lee got up, went to the bathroom.

Uncle Chuck got this serious look on his face. "Lee's gonna stay over."

"Okay." I thought it was better if he didn't drive, the beer and all. "I'm cool on the couch?"

He smiled. "No, Lee sleeps here often."

I forced a smile. "Oh... so—"

"He's my partner."

I heard the toilet flush. Nodded, the shock felt like a punch in my stomach. I had no clue what to say. A rug commercial was playing, the song was super cheery.

Lee sat back on the sofa. "So, did ya tell him?"

Uncle Chuck nodded. "You okay, Randy?"

"Yeah, fine." I looked at the TV wondering what to do. It's wasn't such a big deal. I wondered if Dad knew?

"Both of your parents know," Uncle Chuck said.

"It's not a big deal," Lee said.

"He's pretty sheltered," Uncle Chuck said.

"I am not." It came out louder than I'd intended.

"See?" Lee smiled. "Kids are different now than they were when we grew up."

"He's not some kid. He's my nephew."

Lee nodded.

I faked a yawn. "I think I'll go to bed now. I'm pretty tired."

Uncle Chuck stood up. "I'll show you your room." We walked back through the kitchen to an area off the family room. He switched an overhead light on. The room was large with nice decorations. The bed seemed huge. There was a bathroom attached, without a door.

"There are fresh towels in the bathroom."

"This is nice," I said.

"I hope we didn't—that you're cool. It's just, well, you're gonna be here for a few weeks. I wanted to wait, but Lee was insistent we tell you."

"How long have you and Lee—"

"Three years. We were friends before. It became something else."

I sat on the bed. "You're the first person I know who's gay."

"Lucky me," he joked. It broke some tension.

"There is this kid in my class, James. Gets made fun of by the jocks. He's really... not anything like you guys."

"I know what you mean."

"I just assumed James is gay. But I also kind of avoid him. Even though we're in all the same classes."

"Sounds about right," Uncle Chuck said. "Listen, you've had a long day. Sleep well."

"Yeah. I'm glad I'm here." I wasn't just saying it for him. I'd meant it.

"Me, too. You need anything, come knock. Your TV's over there." He showed me how the remote worked. "We'll get your phone hooked up after breakfast. I'm making berry pancakes. We pick the berries on our farm."

"Yum." I wondered if Lee lived there when I wasn't around.

"Give me a hug," he said. "Good night, Randy."

"Night." Once he'd left, I sat in bed, looked around the room. What would Bear think? My eyes got heavy so I snuggled into the cozy bed, and fell into a deep sleep.

Dinah Won't You Blow

Dinah woke up grouchy. She lay there, listening to the sounds of the coffee grinder in the kitchen. Elroy had probably been up for two hours already. Well, if his insomnia kept him awake, she'd slept through it. Slowly she donned her terrycloth bathrobe, the one that Elroy called her walking bedspread.

"I had the strangest dream," she said, joining him on the threadbare sofa that begged to be replaced.

"Not again," Elroy said. He thumbed through his latest edition of Auto Mechanics while devouring a massive bowl of Wheaties.

She waited until he looked up. "Remember I told you about that new lady at work? Mrs. Kemp?"

"Vaguely." His memory wasn't shot; Dinah was a nurse at Angels' Rest Nursing Home, and she spoke often about her patients: Mrs. Poon who did incessant laps around the circular floor like she was on a treadmill; or Mr. Kallaway who mistook Dinah for his granddaughter, killed in Vietnam.

"Well, in my dream, Mrs. Kemp was teaching a workshop." She paused. "Are you listening, Elroy? For God's sake, I work all day with people I can't communicate with."

He put the magazine down. "Sorry, hon! Don't get your panties in a bunch. You were teaching a workshop?" He took another huge mouthful of cereal.

Dinah blew on her coffee, and then sipped some. "What I said was, Mrs. Kemp was teaching a workshop. I was in the audience."

"Huh. What kind of workshop?"

"Self-esteem." She sipped more coffee.

He waited. "Is there more?"

"Everybody there had low self-esteem. And Mrs. Kemp was explaining how people, just regular folks like you and me, are all the walking wounded. So, you had to choose an unwanted circumstance from your life. I picked my job."

"Good thing you didn't pick us!" Elroy chuckled, popping an Entenmann's doughnut into his mouth.

"Next, we all sat in a semi-circle watching this volunteer, turns out was Cliff Simonds, my neighbor in grade school. And, he's screaming and wailing. And I thought, I'm not going through that!"

"I don't blame you," Elroy grinned.

"Well, then, Mrs. Kemp says to me you're next! And then I woke up."

He patted her leg. "It's just a dream, honey." He grabbed another doughnut.

"Do you think I have low self esteem, Elroy?" Dinah wasn't even sure how to determine if she did. Sure, periodically she chewed the skin off the insides of her thumbs until they were raw. And there were times, at the gym, or the grocery checkout, when she'd glance around to see if others were looking at her. But didn't everybody?

"I wouldn't worry your pretty little head about it," Elroy said. "Nobody's forcing you to go to some asinine workshop." He returned to his magazine.

Dinah sighed.

Every Friday Dinah had lunch with her best friend, Nadine. During their meal, Dinah mentioned her dream.

Nadine said, "I'd just let it go. I don't see how you can work all day in that cuckoo place. It's perfectly normal to dream about it."

Dinah scowled. "Well, I don't see how you can touch complete strangers."

Nadine was a massage therapist at a health club. "Piece of cake, honey," she said, stirring the Equal into her refilled iced tea. "They're called boundaries."

"Do you think I have low self-esteem?"

Nadine pushed back against the banquette. "Why do you ask?"

"Just because."

"Well, since high school, I'd say we've both changed a lot."

"Yeah, I asked Elroy this morning."

"And what did he say?"

"Not to worry my pretty little head about it."

"Ugh. Sounds like Elroy, he can be so…"

"Whatever, Nadine. This isn't about him. Answer me." She heard desperation in her voice.

The waiter placed the check on the table.

Nadine waited. "Why does my opinion matter?"

Dinah pondered why it was so important. She often dreamt about one of the patients.

Normally it didn't bother her.

Finally Nadine spoke. "I'd say you have average self-esteem. Perfectly normal."

"That's just the thing." Dinah's eyes filled with tears. "I don't feel normal."

Nadine took Dinah's hand. "Hey, it's okay," she said, patting it. 'I'm sure it's nothing. Are you working on your poetry lately?"

"No." Dinah glanced at her watch. "Oh shit! I'm late for work!"

Dinah worked the 1-9 shift. She preferred it, because by the time she'd arrive, the patients were heavily medicated. Today she almost ran into Mrs. Poon doing her laps. Mr. Faber was slumped over the nurses desk, protesting.

"Don't blame me, I wasn't the one who took it."

"I know, I know," Dinah replied, leading Mr. Faber back to

the recreation room. *Dick Van Dyke* reruns were playing on the large screen TV.

"Hi Dinah," Mrs. Storm, another patient, said.

"Hello honey," Dinah said, a little surprised at her clarity.

"It was him—he took it!" Mr. Faber said, as he sat.

"Liar!" said Mr. DiCrasto, his roommate. He pointed at him. "He's lying again. Been at it all morning. Get me out of here. I can't stand liars!"

"Now, there, boys. Let's try to get along, okay?" Dinah knew it made no sense to get involved in their dynamics. She walked back to the desk so that the morning nurse, Sonia, could give Dinah her notes. They went over the med schedule, visitations, the log book.

Suddenly, out of nowhere, Sonia asked, "Have you been crying?"

"No, why?"

"Your eyeliner is screwed up. It's usually perfect."

Dinah had used Maybelline since high school, could apply it with her eyes closed. She looked into the office mirror, fluffed her hair. "I had to rush this morning. Elroy took forever in the bathroom."

"Oh," Sonia said. She looked back at the chart.

"Sonia, can I ask you something? Promise you'll be honest?"

"Okay."

"Do you think that I have low self-esteem?"

"Um, I never really gave it any thought, Dinah. I'm not sure. Is everything all right with Elroy?"

"Oh, God, yeah. Same as ever. I just had this weird dream last night. When I woke up it felt like I…well…like I don't know who I am. Has that ever happened to you?"

"Not that I can recall. Sometimes I wake up and forget where I am. Like, a second."

They stared at one another.

"I'm sure it's nothing, just a dream," Dinah said. "You'd better hit the road."

"Yeah, okay, see you tomorrow." Sonia patted her shoulder. "Hang in there!"

Dinah reapplied her liner, then took a walk around the floor. Everyone was napping except patients watching TV, and Mrs. Poon. Dinah did a room check. In her two years at Angels' Rest, she'd witnessed some strange events. Everyone had some form of dementia: Alzheimer's, head traumas, and many were just senile.

At one doorway, she stopped. There was a young, black man sitting in a chair, reading to Mr. Sweeny, who was lying in bed. Dinah craned her neck to hear. It sounded like it might be poetry. She tiptoed into the room, not wanting to startle the man, whose back was to the door.

He turned, reaching into his coat pocket, and saw her. "Oh, hi," he whispered.

Dinah noticed two things. Mr. Sweeny was lightly snoring, and this was the closest she'd ever been to a black person. Alone. Well, sort of, if you didn't count the patients. She held out her hand. "Hi, I'm the nurse. Name's Dinah."

He shook her hand. His smile seemed to come from inside his eyes. "Dinah won't you blow? Like the song?"

She retracted her hand, feeling her face flush. "That's not funny."

He looked surprised. "Hey...I didn't mean..."

"No, it's okay." She took a step backward.

"Sorry, no offense meant. It just popped into my head."

"It's okay. When I was little, kids.... I've heard it a million times."

"Well, my name's Rodney. Imagine the kind of shit I get for that!"

They laughed. His teeth were incandescent, a dazzling contrast to his dark skin.

"So, what's that you're reading to Mr. Sweeny?"

"Oh, this? It's *Leaves of Grass*." He handed her the paperback book.

"Walt Whitman." She studied the photograph on the front. "A poet?"

"One of the finest. We're studying him in class."

189

"Cool." She handed the book back to him. "Do you write any poetry?"

Rodney chuckled. "I try. Some days are better than others."

"I know," Dinah nodded. "I'm kind of a closet poet, too."

"Really? A fellow poet? My homies think I'm a fool."

Suddenly Dinah's heart beat faster. "Want to hear something I wrote recently?" She shocked herself.

"Okay."

She led Rodney toward the nurse's station. As they rounded the corner, Mr. Faber was standing there again.

"I didn't do it," Mr. Faber said, holding his hands up as if he was being arrested. "He took it," he continued, pointing at Rodney.

"What's on TV?" Dinah said to him. "Let's go see." She escorted Mr. Faber back to the rec. room where *All My Children* was playing. While she and Rodney walked back to the office, she asked whether he was related to Mr. Sweeny.

"Nope, no relation. I just read to a different person every Friday on my lunch hour."

They sat at the white formica table in the office.

Rodney looked around. "Is it okay that I'm in here?"

"You're not going to mug me, are you?" Dinah joked. Rodney laughed again. "So, what brings you to Angels' Rest? I mean, if you aren't related to anyone here."

190

"I came to meet you," Rodney said, raising an eyebrow.

She laughed. "Yeah, right." If only Nadine could see her now. "Want some Fritos?"

"Nah, I already ate, thanks. Actually, I've been coming here almost a year now. Either here or St. Mary's, but the staff there are... kind of uptight."

"Really?" Dinah dug into the Fritos bag, took out a handful.

"Just a vibe, but the energy's better here. More relaxed."

Dinah laughed. That wasn't a word she'd use to describe work. She retrieved her journal from her backpack. "How come I've never seen you here before?"

He shrugged and Dinah noticed his massive shoulders. "I've seen you. Even said hello more than once."

Could this be true? Did she simply pass people by, not paying attention? She stuffed some Fritos in her mouth and chewed them. "Well, the ward can be busy sometimes."

"That's why I try to find the quietest room. Mr. Sweeny's. Or Mrs. Hoverman's. They just lie there while I read. Sometimes Mrs. Hoverman hums, or makes little gurgling noises."

"She does?" She wiped her hands on her pants, and turned to one of her most recent poems. "Okay, I wrote this poem about a month ago."

"Hit me."

She cleared her throat, smiled weakly. "Would you rather just read it?" He shook his head, nope. "Okay, here goes nothing. It's untitled."

> "In a frozen
> crystal
> tear
> you suddenly
> reappear
> dripping
> rolling
> toward my mouth
>
> I taste
> your salt
> like a wound
> like a weapon
> I could never
> bring myself
> to use…"

She stopped and looked up. Rodney had his eyes closed. She waited, crossing her legs.

She cleared her throat, thought about grabbing more Fritos.

"Wow," he said, finally. Nodded. He took her hands and stared into her eyes. "That was really something."

She squirmed a little. He smelled faintly of tuna fish. "Thanks!"

"Some heavy emotional pain in that poem, man. I'm impressed."

She wasn't sure what to say. She tried to look at his lips, but that conjured images of them kissing her entire body. "Rodney."

He grabbed a sheet of paper and scribbled something. "There's an open mic night at this café on Wednesday night. I've been going on and off for a while. Want to meet me there?"

"What time?" She forced the thought of Elroy out of her mind. At least for now.

"Starts at eight."

She shrugged. "Sure."

"And I'm going to call you Di from now on. Like Lady Di." He stood.

"Isn't that kind of tragic? I mean, with what happened to her and all?"

"Not if you think about how inspiring she was to so many people."

"Okay, I guess."

"Thanks for reading your poem. I've got to get back to school. My 2:00 class is Literature from the 1800s. We just read Pride and Prejudice." He lingered in the doorway. "Great book."

She stood and noticed he seemed suddenly taller. "Yes, I loved Sense and Sensibility. How old are you, Rodney?"

"Old enough to know," he said, with a wink. That smile. "See you Wednesday."

The days flew by, and finally Wednesday arrived. As luck would have it, every Wednesday, Elroy met a couple of his hunting buddies at Indoor Archery. He usually went straight from the office. Dinah invited Nadine, who came over to her house so they could car pool to the reading.

"Wow, hot mama," Nadine said.

Dinah had purchased a new satiny black blouse at T.J. Maxx, and wore tight black and white striped low-waisted pants with a wide patent leather belt. There was a subtle line of flesh revealed at her belly. "Is it too much?" she asked, sliding on strapless sandals.

"Does the pope shit in the woods?" Nadine joked.

Dinah ran a brush through her hair. "I'm nervous. I've never read my poems at one of these things."

Nadine sat on her counter. "Well, if it's any consolation, you've done karaoke about a thousand times."

"Yeah, but I was always three sheets to the wind!"

Nadine laughed. "That's true, but you'll do great. How'd you hear about this?"

"A guy at work." Dinah added another layer of Maybelline eyeliner.

"Terry?" He was one of the part-time nurses that Nadine had dinner with. Once.

"Nope. A guy who reads to the patients."

"Like a candy striper?"

"Nadine, please, that's archaic. He's just a...volunteer. We'd better go, I want to get there a little early so we can get good

194

seats." She fluffed her hair and pursed her lips in the mirror.

"Relax! It's not like we're going to a Justin Bieber concert."

When they arrived at Dragonfly Café, Dinah noticed Rodney standing with friends on the outdoor patio. She pretended she didn't see him. Nadine ordered chamomile tea, as Dinah stared at the menu. Suddenly she felt two hands on her hips.

"Di!" a voice said in her ear. "You came."

A rush went through her body as she turned. "Hey, Rodney. This is my best friend, Nadine."

He held out his hand and Nadine took it. "Pleasure to meet you."

"Likewise." Nadine said, grinning.

Dinah noticed Nadine's lipstick stained her teeth.

Rodney turned her hand over and stared at it. "You work with your hands, don't you?"

"You're perceptive," Nadine said. "As a matter of fact, I do."

Dinah's stomach lurched. Was it jealousy? No! "I'll have a white mocha latte."

"The chocolate ones are better," Rodney offered.

"I'll stick with my order, but thanks anyhow."

"Suit yourself. Join us at my table when you have your drinks."

He pointed to the largest table in the center of the cafe. "Sign up to read. And don't be nervous, Di."

"I won't be. I mean… I'm not." She noticed he'd picked out his fro, and he looked like Lenny Kravitz. A glow surrounded his head from the lights. He nodded, then pivoted. They both watched as he joined his friends outside.

"Who the hell was that stud?"

Dinah looked around. "Nadine, lower your voice. My God, this isn't Benny's Tavern. It's a poetry reading, for chrissakes."

"All I'm saying is Rodney's H-O-T. And you're on fire. What's going on? Out with it, missy."

"Nothing. He's the guy I met at work." Nadine looked clueless. "The one who comes in and reads to patients."

"Uh huh. Nothing to tell? Dinah, you're full of shit. If I had a match, I could have lit you on fire when he was standing here."

They walked to the large table and sat down. "Oh, pul-lease, Nadine. You think everyone is out trying to get laid all the time? If you recall, I have a boyfriend. And if you must know, Rodney and I spoke about poetry and literature. Not your everyday conversation. That's it."

Nadine looked over her shoulder at the patio. "So you're telling me you don't find him attractive?"

"That's not the point."

"Okay, because you remember our rule. The one we had before Elroy. If you're not interested, then he's fair game."

Dinah tried to picture Nadine with Rodney. "He's only twenty, for chrissakes."

"Yeah, so? Did ya ever see Rosemary's Baby? Oops, I mean, that other movie, from the sixties with Dustin Hoffman and Anne whats-her-name?"

"I believe it's called The Graduate. And yes, I've seen it. Here comes Rodney and his pals. Behave yourself."

The open mic event began. The host was a strange fellow with a pompadour, who began reading a selection from a 1950s Emily Post etiquette book. Rodney was next. Just before his name was called he whispered to Dinah, "Wish me luck." He strode to the mic with confidence.

"This poem is called Crossing Over at Babylon…

Foliage. Greenery so dense,
So plush
Against the blue sky backdrop
Freshly manicured
Postage stamp lawns
Surrounding ranch style
Duplicity
All eyes cast to stone
And the horizontal line
Of the speed of movement
Becomes curiously disguised
In the murderous element
We call Mankind
For what kind of men are these
Of which I am one
Searching for some affirmation
Seeking to ease the pain of
Unrealized insecurities

The ache to belong
Belief in fiction
In truths lived outside
The self
The insatiable pleasure seekers
Giving up skins
Riding high
Without soul…"

Rodney smiled as everyone clapped. Nadine leaned over to Dinah and whispered, "Wow, that was cool. I didn't get it, did you?"

Dinah was loading the dishwasher. "Do people have souls?" she asked Elroy.

"How the heck do I know? Did you notice we're out of Wheaties?"

"I'm serious."

"So am I, hon. I eat them every day for breakfast."

"What about when people say they're soul partners?" She couldn't help herself.

"Is this more of that Nadine crap? Is she filling your head with this nonsense?"

"For your information, Nadine is smarter about certain things than you."

He snorted and crossed his arms. "Okay, Dinah. You're talking about a massage therapist who barely finished high school. It's just downright silly to compare her intelligence to mine."

"Yes, this, coming from someone who gets enjoyment out of shooting innocent deer. I didn't say anything about intelligence. There's a difference between book smarts and life experience, Elroy. You might interrupt your fishing show on TV long enough to live a little."

He mumbled "Whatever" under his breath, and turned to walk away.

"And Elroy?" He stopped, barely turned. "Get your own Wheaties."

Two days later, Rodney was at Angels' Rest again. She found him reading to Mrs. Hoverman in a corner of the dining room. Dinah took a seat and waited for him to come to a break.

"What's that you're reading?" she asked.

"Poems by Rumi. Ever heard of him?"

"That's bullshit!" said Mrs. Hoverman. The intensity made Dinah jump.

"Yeah," she lied. "Heard of him. Not sure which poems though. Like, I don't think I'd know one, like "Two Roads Diverged…""

"In a yellow wood…" Rodney continued.

Their eyes locked. The world stopped.

"What's going on? I feel like…like…"

"Shhh," he said, putting his finger up to her lips. He looked to see if Mrs. Hoverman was paying attention, but her head was on her chest and she was drooling. "Come on," he motioned.

Dinah followed him to the office area behind the nurses desk. Her stomach was in a knot, and she noticed her breathing felt shallow.

"Your friend called me the day after the poetry reading."

"Nadine?" she asked, even though she knew.

"Uh huh. She read me a poem of hers on the phone, one she'd written that night."

"Oh," Dinah said, reaching for a chart. Nadine had read the same poem to her first. It was an ode to her uterus, and mentioned several more body parts. Plus the ocean, ebb and flow. Thinking about it now made Dinah blush.

"I told her that I wasn't interested." Rodney reached over and took the chart out of her hands. "It's your poetry I want to hear, Di."

"Um," Dinah wasn't sure what to say. She could hear someone outside the office yelling "Get Me Out Of Here!" She attempted to smile at Rodney, who took her hand and slowly massaged it. "I should tell you that I live with someone."

"I know."

"You do?" Figures Nadine would tell him, she thought.

200

"It doesn't matter, Di. No one knows you like I do."

Was this happening? His arms were slowly going around her body, pulling her against him. She felt his youthful eagerness, and before she knew it his lips pressed hers, waiting for her tongue to meet his.

"Wait! Rodney…" She pulled slowly away, feeling intoxicated. Rodney held her, not letting her go. "I'm, I'm…" She searched for the words. "White."

He looked surprised. "White?" He grinned. "No shit," he said. "And I'm colorblind."

She laughed, the tension of the moment settling. "Do people have souls?"

He closed his eyes and brought her close to him again. She smelled leather from his coat, and Irish Spring soap, and his chest was hard. He felt really good.

"Sure they do," he said. "Can't you feel mine?"

She waited a moment, holding him there. "I think so. You?"

"Oh yeah, Di. I felt yours the moment we met. Yours is poetry in motion."

I WAS DON HO'S HO

It isn't a mistake, and I know what you're thinking. Because although there is some irony in that Don LOVED Ho-ho's, I still meant what I said—I was Don Ho's ho; not Don's Ho-ho. He enjoyed Ho-ho's so much he would eat them at 3 a.m. He'd store them in the garage, the basement, the attic. He liked them with Skippy's and Cool-Whip. Have you ever microwaved them? Take my advice, don't.

You know the Don I'm talking about, right? The one-hit wonder who sang Tiny Bubbles? Betcha didn't know that song was about me.

We met at his second wedding. I'd been invited to join my best pal, Sukie. We flew for Aloha Airlines, and she grew up with Don's cousin. I swear, everybody's related in Hawaii. It's just one humungous gene pool. I stood at the food table eyeing the pastrami finger sandwiches, cut into fours like my mother did when I was little. One second, Sukie was beside me. Yet when I turned to face her, I was glancing down on the groom's head.

Instantly I realized that I was about six inches taller than him (we'll get to the Napolean Complex later). I fixated on his cowlick. I have a theory about cowlicks. I've noticed that people with cowlicks often have other strange patterns, like predatory, or indecisiveness, in their lives. Serial killers are notoriously cowlick growers. Also senior VPs of major oil companies.

I was torn between the Mahi Mahi or the Whipped Fruit Salad. Then I noticed the tray with the cloves of baked garlic all laid out like clumps of bee poop. When I reached out for one, so did Don. Our hands collided like two football tight ends. And just like that, Don broke my wrist. My initial reaction was that my calcium supplement let me down.

Later he'd joke about it, like he didn't know how powerful he was. But that day he insisted on escorting me to Kahuna Memorial. I must have been in shock because I said okay. I completely forgot this was Don Ho's wedding day. Then, nobody could find Sukie to save my life. Turns out, she'd disappeared with one of her sex buddies, a man named Palani who we just called Lonny. Every Hawaiian that I know has a double name, and leads two lives.

On the way to the hospital, in the back of his limo, Don sang something cheesy. He repeated each chorus completely in Hawaiian words. He tried to cheer me up but it made me even crazier, hearing such limited consonants. All those k's, h's, l's grated on me. The bagged ice helped to numb the pain, but leaked all over my Donna Karan serape. I wanted to slap him, or at the very least, tell him to shut up.

At the hospital, they gave me all sorts of pain meds. And that was kind of nice. I'm one of those people who forever helped herself to friends leftover pain pills. For instance, when my friend, Katie broke her leg skiing at Snowbird, she saved me the rest of her Nembutal. I'd go through complete strangers' medicine cabinets. Even before we'd arrived at Kahuna Memorial I was banking on some good pills to mix later with tequila or daquiris. When they said I'd have to wear a cast, I freaked. Don apparently felt completely awful, as you can imagine. I wanted to sign my name Mrs. Ho on the hospital release form. But then I thought if there was the slightest chance I could sue the poor bastard that might not help in court.

As they applied the last plaster of paris, Sukie suddenly showed up, and sometime around then, Don split. When she gets nervous, Sukie expels gas. I knew this from working with her in tight spaces, like the kitchen compartment of 737s. I only hoped that she wouldn't fart now that we were alone. God forbid the doctor, who looked a little like Richard Chamberlain in The Thorn Birds, might think it was me.

Don called me the next day, and the next day after that. He was relentless. When he would stop by, I'd usually go for a drive with him. I couldn't work, so all my time was free. To avoid him, I'd go to the beach, getting there early enough so that the surfer dudes would see my cast.

"Gnarly, dude!" they'd say. I'd smile in my two piece Jantzen suit, sipping my first batch of margaritas with my good hand. "Surf's up, shaka!" I'd watch their tight asses jutting like two cantaloupes out of their wetsuits as they carried their surfboards into the water.

Some days Sukie would join me. We'd go to the Halikalani Hotel pool. Sukie knew the hotel manager, Kamala, so we had free access. She did those early morning workout routines along with the television. Her body was a knockout and it worked like a magnet. We'd play this game called Married, Divorced, Single or Gay. Each hotel guest had to fit one category or another, even if we thought they might be married, and gay, for instance. That day, there were plenty of potential crossovers.

"Oh, there's Don Ho," she said. She poked me with her hand, which looked about eighty from too much sun.

I turned, and everything was kind of fuzzy from the Percodan. "Big deal."

"Honey, get with it. He's a big deal. It's only you howlies who poke fun."

"Spare me, Sukie. You were the one who said he has a Napolean Complex." Basically, Sukie had explained, he was like

204

those jack terrier dogs, big dogs inside a little dogs' body. And I could see how that was true, the way he strutted over like a prize fighter, like Ali.

Don said hello. He was wearing a ridiculous Hawaiian shirt that was about five sizes too big and white Ray-Bans. It was the Speedo that hooked me. I have a thing for bathing suits that go up people's cracks. Go figure. I just think it takes, well, balls.

"Hey, ladies, want some company?" He sat down before either of us could respond.

"Hi, Don. You've got something…" Sukie pointed to her mouth. I looked and sure enough, Don had a smear of chocolate on the edge of his. The ho-ho addict. He wiped it off with a flowered handkerchief. I wondered if he had a stash in the hotel somewhere.

Sukie excused herself to use the bathroom. We both watched her flounce off.

"Why so glum, Don?" I twirled the fuscia umbrella stuck in my Maitai. I was a little irritated because he'd interrupted our game when it had only just started.

He shrugged. "My wife's a bitch."

"Why'd you marry her then?"

"No alternative." It was the first time he let down that ridiculous public persona, and I felt for him. But I also thought of my dickless husband who, feeling a similar lack of alternatives, had jumped from the Na Pali cliffs last year. I hadn't dated anyone since. I couldn't bear to have someone that could remind me of him every day.

I smiled at Don. "You ride your Harley here?"

He grinned, and he did have nice teeth. There were some good dentists in Honolulu. "Yup."

When Sukie came back, we told her we'd go pick up some Tequila and pomegranate juice. It was lots cheaper to mix your own, and the Halekalani pool staff never said anything, even if they knew.

On the back of his Harley, holding on to Don, I felt a sudden kinship. And he had the tiniest love handles. I told him that in aisle seven and he whooped and slapped his thigh. He decided to get champagne instead of tequila. Don was cheap, and they had a special on Brut. And when we poured it poolside, between the chaise lounges, he said, "Look at all the tiny bubbles!" As if it was his first damn time drinking champagne or something.

The last time I combined champagne and pain meds, I got the silly notion to wind surf into Waimea Canyon. It was a windy winter day and I had no fear as I left the ledge. It was better than any ride at Disneyworld. Better than the Ice Capades on mescaline. It was nirvana.

After some time, when the buzz kicked in fully, I leaned over to Don, careful to lift my cast in the air. He'd replaced Sukie on her lounge. Through thick lips, I whispered in his ear, "I wanna be your ho."

Surprised, he took my cast, and gently kissed it. "Okay."

Jesus Votives

We were putting on our clothes following an afternoon screw, the light filtering into the room through the transparent curtains. I sneezed suddenly, and wiped my face on the sleeve of my work shirt. I didn't think she'd notice.

"Gross! How about Kleenex? Never mind, don't even answer that. You know those frappucinos from Starbucks that you have about eight times a day? Well, you'd be a lot less phlegmy if you stopped drinking them."

"Huh?" I was still trying to see if there was any obvious remaining snot left on my shirt.

"Not to mention the amount of money you'd save in a year—imagine! We could actually take a vacation. Go to Lake Champlain!"

She had even less of an idea where that was than I did. "Just get your clothes on and let's get out of here. You're starting to sound like my wife."

"Ex-wife last time I checked. And is there a reason why you still wear that ring?"

I sighed.

We'd met during the 4:40 showing of *Something About Mary*. I was feeling really low at work, so I left early, ducking into the closest theater. There were only six other people in the Quad Cinema on 13th Street and she sat in the row directly behind me.

When it got to the part where Cameron Diaz introduces her "special" brother to Matt Dillon, I heard her say, "Ohmigod! Goofy bastard!" And even though I was a little appalled, she leaned closer, and whispered in my left ear, "He looks just like my boss," which raised my curiosity. I tried to figure out if she worked with special people, or meant Matt Dillon.

When the movie ended, she stood, held out her hand and said, "I'm Karla. I'm going to El Rey Del Sol for margaritas, wanna come?" Without waiting for an answer, she turned and walked away. I really didn't make a choice, not then. I just followed until we were standing outside the theater.

She lit a cigarette. Her thick, blonde hair glistened in the set-ting sun, that slanting kind of autumn light that reminded me of bales of straw. "So, whaddya think?" She took a long drag and blew the smoke out of the corner of her mouth.

I shrugged. I often go to movies alone. I wasn't used to discuss-ing them. "It was a little, well…" I had trouble finding even one word to summarize it all.

"Goofy?" she asked, smiling a grin that made me smile back. "C'mon," she said, linking her arm through mine. The impact of her movement carried us both forward, and I was swept to-ward 14th Street and El Rey Del Sol.

"Ever been here before?" Karla asked, as we were led through the tiny restaurant to an even smaller patio in an alley behind the kitchen.

We sat, and I looked up at the various apartment buildings looming around us. "No, I live across town."

"Brooklyn?" she said, with a faint air of disdain, like I was some piece of shit if I lived over a bridge or through a tunnel.

"No, the East Village."

"Hmm." She gave me a once over. "You don't look the type."

I sort of half-smiled. I'd heard this many times before: one version of it or another. You look like a Kennedy. Or, do you come from money? Women often tried to carve some myth out of my location. And who cares, right? I say let them!

Karla lit up again. "I like this place 'cause you can smoke. Even wacky weed. And the drinks come in these Jesus candles." She demonstrated with her hands, but I was clueless. "Ya don't know Jesus candles?" She started listing off the most common margarita flavors. "Usually they've got cantaloupe, banana, pineapple, and coconut. Then there's a flavor-of-the-day. What day is it, Thursday? Might be kiwi!"

I have to admit, her childish enthusiasm was amusing. Before our kiwi margarita's had even arrived, I knew I was gonna get laid.

I told her I was an accountant, to which she added, "What a hoot!" I was somewhat afraid to ask what she did for work. When I did, she replied, "I book clowns."

The drinks arrived.

"You...what?" I'd never heard of that before.

"Yeah, clowns, like Ronald McDonald? We have several professional clowns who do everything—entertain people at carnivals, act on TV commercials, go to birthday parties. We keep them pretty busy." She sipped her margarita. Well, more like gulped.

"And you're their booker?"

She nodded. "It's a cake job. I've been with the company since college. Just can't leave. I'm too attached to those clowns." She laughed, so I did, too. "I know, crazy isn't it?"

"No." I shook my head emphatically, trying not to think about my wife, who'd left six months earlier. Karla's inability to leave her clowns suddenly made her look like a prize to me. I smiled a big grin at this clown booker.

"You have any siblings?" I asked, wiping a dribble of kiwi juice from my mouth.

"Yeah, my older brother's HIV positive. He owns a tattoo shop in the Mission." Her voice got smaller. "San Francisco. That's where we grew up."

"I'm sorry." I didn't know what to else to say so I looked at my feet and wished I'd worn something other than my tasseled Cole Haan loafers.

"Hey, man, no sweat. He's a survivor. It's been something like ten years since he was diagnosed." She paused. "My little brother's in the clinker." She narrowed her already slanting eyes. "I know," she snorted, "ya gotta wonder which is worse, huh?"

"Really? Gosh, Karla, I'm…"

"He fucked up. He got caught doing what lots of executives and presidents and all sorts of hoity-toity people do."

I wondered what his crime was—murder? "What's he in for?"

"He was working for the mob. An inside job. And they made him the fall guy, or at least that's what he says. He wasn't willing to blow the whistle on his loser buddies, so he got twenty years, booked for armed robbery with attempted murder." She lit a cigarette, blew out the match. "Enough about me, how about you?"

I was reluctant to disclose any details about my family after that. "Well, I've only got one younger sister. She's working on her master's at Columbia. Journalism."

"Wow, she must be smart. Smarter than you, I'll bet!" she joked, and the pressure drained away. "Listen, you wanna get out of here?"

She'd already pounded her entire margarita, and I was only half finished with mine. But I had reason to think that something better was coming, so I said, "Sure."

In the elevator up to my floor, she said, "So, you still married?"

"Nope," I lied. Technically we were, although only on paper. I hadn't seen hide nor hair of Carissa since March when she went to do the laundry and never returned. Called me from New Mexico to tell me it was over. She'd met someone. I should have seen it coming, could have predicted the ulcer that followed. My parents "told you so" attitude didn't help matters. The work-appointed therapist, Dr. Harriet Montague, sided with Carissa's perspective so often that I wondered if they had phone sessions in between our appointments. When I'd mention that, the doctor would say, "The paranoia is just a side effect of your depression." Or other reassuring statements like, "Your depression was there way before Carissa. Possibly since childhood." I stopped seeing her and never told anyone.

"Hello?" Karla jabbed me in the stomach.

I grunted, not realizing I'd drifted quite so much.

"You going to answer my question?"

"Sorry, what was it again?" The elevator opened to the 6th floor and I stepped out, toward my flat.

"If you're divorced, then why are you still wearing that ring?" she said to my back.

I stopped in front of my door, and turned around. "You ask too many questions," I said, leaning closer into her face.

"Enquiring minds want to—"

I stopped her with a full kiss on her mouth, the taste of cigarettes mixed with juicy fruit gum and kiwi. It worked; she shut up. I lifted her around and pressed her against my front door. As our lips locked, I slid my arms around her thighs and hoisted her off the floor. Our energy was swirling as our tongues explored each other's mouths. Her legs wrapped tighter around my waist. This was my first kiss in six months and I felt she sensed it as I grinded against her.

Suddenly she pulled her head away, wiped her mouth and nodded past me. I lowered her to the carpet and turned around slowly.

"Hi, Mr. Walters!" It was my neighbor in 6F, four-year-old Dexter Ramsey.

"Hi Dexter," I said. I reached into my pocket to locate my keys.

Dexter raised his little hand. "Hi, Mrs. Walters!"

I looked at Karla, dismayed, but she lit up. "Hello there, Dexter!" She leaned down to him in slow motion. "I haven't seen you in so long, how are you?"

I couldn't open that door fast enough.

The first thing she noticed was the bird. I'd bought it the week that Carissa moved out.

I'd never owned a pet before, and my buddy at work, Harris, recommended it. He said reptiles or birds were the easiest pets.

"What's its name?" Karla asked. She stood in front of the cage, in a corner of my narrow kitchen.

"I just call it Birdie," I said, feeling my face flush a little.

"Hey Birdie," she said, jiggling a bell attached to a mirror on the side of the cage. "Boy or girl?"

I shrugged. "No clue. Any guesses?"

"Does she shit a lot?"

I laughed. "Not any more then we do. Well, most of us, I guess." Boy, I was really striking out. I guess I was more nervous now that she was inside my place. Somehow the hallway was more conducive to this being a fantasy. I stared at her fantastic ass.

"Mind if I look around?" she asked, as she pushed past me.

I wondered what she might find. An empty candy wrapper on the floor? One of the girlie magazines I'd bought months ago. Again, a Harris suggestion. I said, "I'll show you around!" We walked through my entire flat, which took about a minute. I ended the tour in the bedroom. She noticed the framed photograph on my bedside table and picked it up.

"You and…the wife?"

I nodded. Dammit, I'd left the picture out. It was taken on a beach in Cancun.

Usually, I kept it inside the drawer in the bedside table, but sometimes when I had insomnia, I'd take it out and stare at it. I forgot to put it away last night. "Yes, that's Carissa."

"She's gorgeous."

I swallowed, and sat quickly on the bed. I hadn't spoken about her with any other woman, well not including my mother, my sister, and the brief encounter with Dr. Montague.

Karla came over to sit beside me on the bed. She took one of my hands in hers. "Do you want to talk about it?"

I looked at our hands; hers was muscular, with blue veins close to the surface. I felt safe with her and it was unexpected. The bird chirped in the kitchen.

"We were expecting our first child. Carissa had a difficult pregnancy, and she had to spend lots of time in bed." Karla nodded, glanced at the bed we sat on. "Oh, not this bed, I moved after she…"

"It's okay, go on."

I took a deep breath and exhaled. Could I do this? "We were at my parents' house in Connecticut for dinner. It was about six weeks before her due date, and my dad, who's a doctor, noticed her eyes weren't tracking normally."

"Sorry, what's tracking mean?" Karla was twisting a strand of her thick hair.

I demonstrated that test cops do when they pull you over for suspicion of drinking and driving. I held a finger in front of her nose, moving it slowly side to side.

"Dad didn't want to freak Carissa out, so he told me in private that night. He urged me to take her to the ER, but I knew she would want to see her own doctor. So, on the drive back to Manhattan I suggested we make an appointment the next morning. I couldn't sleep all night, expecting the worse. The next morning, during the ultrasound, our gynecologist couldn't detect a heartbeat."

"Oh, Adam," Karla whispered. I felt her hand on my lower back.

"Turned out the baby's umbilical cord wrapped around its neck. So, Carissa had to deliver it stillborn." I felt mechanical saying these words, until I looked at Karla and saw a tear streaming down her face.

"Was it a little boy or girl?"

"Boy," I said weakly. I closed my eyes, barely able to remember those days.

Karla was crying harder now, making little strangled sounds like an asthmatic. "I'm sorry...I'm so...sorry," she attempted. "Give...me...a minute." I searched for Kleenex, but settled for toilet paper, and she blew her nose, wiped her eyes. "Do you want me to go?"

"No," I sat down beside her, putting my arm around her. "I'm the one who's sorry, such a sad sack. I probably should have waited until we knew each other a little better."

"That's horseshit. Can I smoke in here?" Karla asked. "Never mind, I want to quit anyhow." She wiped her eyes. "Wow-that's so sad. And I thought my life was sad. Guess it's all perspective, huh?"

I put my arm around her. Kissed her on the cheek, noticing a beauty mark for the first time. And as I thought, she really is beautiful, she smiled that sunny grin at me.

Her eyes looked so clearly into mine that it was almost intimidating.

"Listen, Adam, there's something I want to tell you also."

I noticed she fidgeted a little. "Okay, shoot."

"Speaking of shooting, let's do a shot first."

"Okay." I knew I had gin, wasn't certain if I had any tequila, which would have been a better choice. Turns out I did have an old bottle of Cuervo Especial I'd bought in duty free on the way back from our honeymoon. I poured two shots while Karla used my bathroom.

"You could really use a decorator," she said, joining me in the living room.

"Needs a lady's touch, perhaps?" I said suggestively, handing her the shot glass. I noticed she'd applied a rose-colored lipstick.

"To Jesus," she proposed as we clinked them together. "Remember? The Jesus candle margaritas at El Rey Del Sol? Well, these are a mini version. Jesus votives!"

"Yeah, okay." There was a slow burn while the alcohol went down my throat. Then a warm sensation, the numbing anesthetic of tequila.

We set our glasses on the sofa table.

Karla looked a little dazed. "They say that tequila makes you horny."

"I've heard that." I smiled and grabbed her, pulling her closer, against me. We began kissing again, as I placed my hands in the small of her lower back. I slipped my hands inside her pants, feeling the luscious curves of her ass. As I moved to the front of her jeans, I began to unfasten her belt.

"Adam, wait!" She took my hand, and stepped back. "I have to tell you something. Please, sit down."

My mind flashed on a parent-teacher conference in 3rd grade. My teacher, Miss Rapp, was concerned because she'd caught me looking up Laurabeth Hunt's skirt. I was so wrapped up in this memory that I didn't think I heard Karla correctly.

"Adam, I haven't always been Karla."

I laughed. Didn't plan to, just came out. "Huh?"

She repeated herself, more deliberately this time. "I wasn't born Karla."

Okay, I heard that. I coughed. It felt like the wind was literally knocked out of me. I waited. And waited.

"I was born Karl."

I knew that my jaw was open, that I was staring at her, and that I couldn't fully comprehend what was happening. Finally I mustered, "Is this a joke?"

"I wish it was. But, no, Adam, not a joke. I'm transgendered."

I jumped up. My gut reaction told me that I was not capable of handling this, but I also couldn't find the words to say 'get out.' So I paced, unable to look at Karla. "I feel duped." Birdie made more peeping noises.

"I understand," Karla said. "But unlike you telling me about what you went through with Carissa, this is not my first time going through this. See, I was born Karla in Karl's body, and the transformation to Karla happened over ten years ago. I'm a woman in every sense now, live it, breathe it, have most of the anatomy in the right places. I just can't have a baby."

"I'm sorry, it's just crazy." I looked at her for the first time since I'd stood.

"Yes, well life is crazy, and like the movie, it's goofy, and sad, and then you die." She stood, and began collecting her things.

"Wait, where are you going?"

"I think I should leave."

"No," I was surprised with myself. "Please, stay."

And to my astonishment, she did. We stayed up nearly all night talking, falling asleep together with the first glint of dawn creeping in. But hours later, when we woke up, I was wrapped around her, holding on to her for dear life.

My Father, Your Mother, Our Breakfast, The Ghost

My Father

The last time he dropped by it was because he thought I had a car jack. Over a year ago. This morning I was tinkering with some spare car parts. My son, Hunter, was kicking a ball around. I heard the driveway gate creak open, looked up and saw my father round the side of the house. He sat on the cement steps.

He lit a Marlboro. "Where's Fern?"

"Sleeping. Hunter, run inside and go upstairs. See if Mommy's awake." She'd been up most of the night, breast-feeding Lacey, our second child.

"But she doesn't like being—" Hunter started.

"Please." My voice firmer than I'd intended. He bolted inside. "Aren't you supposed to be at work?"

Dad exhaled. "I dropped by on my way."

I stopped fussing with the car, but didn't move closer. Wondered if he'd already been at his bar. I could see he hadn't shaved. He looked haggard. The smoke hung in the air between us like a specter. "What's the special occasion?"

He pulled out a crinkled newspaper page. Handed it to me. "I found her."

I scanned both sides, read headlines. Clueless, I shrugged. "Found who?"

"Flip it back over, the bottom right story."

As I located it, the hairs stood up on my neck. A spooky feeling swept over me and I felt like I could barf.

"I thought you'd both want to know," my father said.

Your Mother

We'd left Milwaukee before the shadow of dawn, while it was completely dark.

Fern was grumpy, jittery. "I still don't want to go," she whined. "I miss the kids."

Cleveland airport, our layover before our flight to Buffalo. "Too late to turn back now. We're halfway there. Why don't you give them another call? Your sister will reassure you they're fine."

We found our next gate. She bit her cuticles, crossed her legs. Uncrossed them. Stared at the image in the newspaper clipping. "What will I say to her?"

I gave it some thought. What would I ask my mom? If I could. "I don't know. Maybe why'd she give you up? Who's your dad? Ya know, questions that matter."

She chewed her lip. "It was easier when I didn't know where she was." Drew a deep breath. "This is scarier than I'd imagined."

"It's going to be okay." I took her hand in mine. "I'm right here every step of the way."

220

Our Breakfast

Fern waited for our bags, while I rented the car. I upgraded to a convertible but it turned out she was too cold exposed to the open air, and we hadn't brought warmer clothes. Just another thing we had poorly planned. We were about halfway to the Cattaraugus Reservation when she blurted, "I'm starving."

We were traversing a rural area, with vast, oblong fields, copses of massive trees. I looked at the GPS and the next sizable town was Perry. "We can stop in about ten." I hadn't noticed, but my stomach was growling. The Perry Dairy had Stewart sandwiches and we sat outdoors on the patio, the only customers. Cicadas buzzed. A humid wind swirled Fern's black hair around.

"You know, you never told me about your mom," she said, attacking her ham and cheese croissant.

I stared at a group of geese settled on the far edge of the lawn. "Not much to tell."

"How old were you, ya know…when she—"

"Five."

I knew what Fern was thinking: I was the same age as Hunter. She'd been patient with me, and now, with what she might have to face about her mother. It was only fair. "The problem is, I only know what my dad has told me. And you know what a reliable source he is."

She nodded, frowned. Kept chewing. "More than I know."

"She drowned." That was easier than I thought.

Fern swallowed hard, pushed her bangs behind one ear. Leaned in. "An accident?"

I shrugged. "Not sure. It happened in the bathtub."

She narrowed her green eyes. "Not...sure?"

I couldn't look at her, pointed at her sandwich. "You going to finish that?"

The Ghost

There are some things that haunt you. Everybody's different. But for us, Fern and me, we shared a common thread. Mothers. Truth was, I'd gone through infinite spells, years even, of not thinking about my mom once. But ever since Lacey was born, it clobbered me. I couldn't sleep. Our little girl's got her nose. Her laugh.

Fern was looking out at the endless fields of corn, the sun shining off the silky husks.

"It's baffling," Fern said. "How huge these fields are. The rows of corn are endless."

I said, "They're the same outside of Milwaukee, if you head north."

She shook her head. "No, not like this. Not like this at all."

Truth is, I'm a little jealous. I'd give anything to have my mother back, but that ghost just won't budge. And now, Fern will meet the mother she never knew. Possibly put her ghost to rest.

Fern dozed, and I stopped the car on the narrow shoulder. I got out, stretched. Walked about fifty paces down the road to a narrow bridge. The water was fast, swirling from recent rains. As I looked at the clouds, wispy mists in the sky, I whispered, "Please, Ma...let me go."

Back on the road, the sign for Cattaraugus Reservation loomed. I slowed the car. "We're here," I said, rubbing the top of her head, nestled against my shoulder.

Fern woke up. "Ever since breakfast," she said, "there's a song stuck in my head. It's by The Psychedelic Furs. I can't remember the name. See if you recognize it?" As she sang, her gorgeous, warbling voice cut through me:

"Inside you the time moves
and she don't fade
the ghost in you
She don't fade..."

Nuts & Bolts

She always waited until the tub was at least half full until she threw the clothes into the washer. Dottie liked to slowly dunk each item into the warm water, and watch as it floated down to the bottom. Often it would bring her back to a time, at age six, when she was swimming in a neighbor's pool. The mothers were at the deep end of the pool, sitting under a patio umbrella, chatting. She dove in, accidentally hitting her head on the concrete bottom. The next few minutes were a blur; she vaguely remembered, with a dream-like quality, a flat, endless white space while floating up to the top. Actually, the neighbor boy, Brad, saw her on the bottom of the pool, dove in, and rescued her.

Lying on the patio, she threw up what felt like the entire pool of water while her mother lavished praise on Brad. She felt so stupid, like it was her fault. And according to her mother, it was.

Today she hummed a Carpenter's tune, "Top of the World." When she got to the chorus, she sang aloud. "Looking... down on creation, and the only explanation I can find..." She always had to go through Lenny's pockets. He was forever leaving things in them and the papers, when wet, would become tiny balls that stuck to her flannel nighties. It made her crazy. "Is the love that I found, ever since you been a..." In his blue Dickies work pants there was a matchbook. Lenny didn't smoke. The cover was chocolate brown edged with colored balloons in the center. Along the bottom it said, 'Be Safe * Keep Cover Closed.'

Dottie giggled. If only she'd had access to matches when she was young. She'd have burned her house down, no doubt. That would have been one way to keep her stepfather's hands off her.

She opened the cover and inside, on the top flap was a name scrawled in pen. It said: Nancy. With a number, 486-2810. Who the hell was Nancy? She felt the air leave the room and collapsed on the floor.

Ten minutes later, which seemed like two hours, she picked up the phone and dialed.

Twirled the cord around her fingers. On the third ring, someone picked up. She hung up before a voice even said hello. What would she say? She felt a mixture of excitement and fear. Prank phone calls from sleepovers in junior high school came to her. Calling the guidance counselor at home, pretending to have swallowed a bottle of aspirin. Calling people whose last names rhymed with swear words. Why would Lenny do this? He was an asshole, that's why.

She dialed the number again.

"Hello?"

The voice sounded young, like a dwarf. "Hello, I'm looking for," she forgot the name and had to look at the matches. "Nancy?"

"Hang on." She heard the phone being set down, then a muffled, "Mom."

Mom? Nancy was a mom? Did Lenny know this? He hated kids. She paced up and down the hallway.

"Y'ello."

"Hi, Nancy, my name's Dottie. How are you?"

"Busy as hell. What can I do for ya?"

"Oh, I'm—" she paused. "—calling to…" Think, Dottie, think. She swallowed. "Know anyone by the name of Lenny?"

A long pause. "Jenny—come and get this dog and take him outside. NOW." The phone was covered, that muffled sound again. She waited. "Yeah, um, what was your name again?"

"Dottie." She debated whether or not to say her last name. Lenny's last name, that rat bastard.

"Listen, Dottie," she sounded as if she was lighting a cigarette. "I know Len, but why should that concern you? Ain't nobody's business but ours."

She wanted to blurt, well, is it your business if he has syphilis? But instead all she muttered was, "I'm his wife."

They met that afternoon at Scrub and Suds Laundromat, the fancy one owned by the Korean family. Dottie got there early, and waited in her Ford Taurus until Nancy showed up. As Nancy ambled toward the back of the store, Dottie was surprised at how old she appeared, how generally unattractive and bent over she was. Dottie imagined she'd be another Pamela Anderson, or some other sex kitten. She turned off the Carpenters Greatest Hits CD, and with a quick close-up look in her rear view mirror, she walked toward the cleaners.

"Nancy?" she said.

The woman turned around. "Hi."

"Help you?" An elderly Korean woman suddenly appeared. "Need quarters?"

"Oh, no, we're just meeting," Dottie said, then laughed awkwardly.

Nancy laughed, too. She lit a Virginia Slim.

The Korean lady laughed too. She said, "Okee dokee," and walked back to the office.

"Let's sit, my ass is tired," Nancy said, blowing out a huge poof of smoke.

Dottie sat down and smoothed her pleated pants. She tried to clear her head.

"I had no idea," Nancy began. "He lied to me."

Dottie looked into Nancy's brown eyes. She saw the truth there. She nodded.

Somehow she already knew this, but hearing it was an entirely different story.

"I'm leaving him." Dottie felt some of her anger rising. "You can have him."

"Not worth the trouble." Nancy flicked her ashes on the floor.

"I was really mad at you." Dottie waved the smoke away. "Before I called."

"I can see why. I'm so sorry. Can I make it up to you?" Nancy asked.

Dottie knew it wasn't entirely Nancy's fault. Still she shook her head no. "Men," she said, swallowing the acidic bile in her throat.

"Fucking men," Nancy agreed through a cloud of smoke.

When she got home, she packed all her belongings in the Ford. She wrote a short note, to the point, and set the matchbook there. Her ring was placed beside their wedding photo that used to adorn the console. The photo was ripped cleanly in half, his face burnt to a crisp.

Nearing Las Vegas, Dottie was transfixed by the neon lights. She'd never been to the big city before, and Reno felt like a cow town in comparison. A friend from high school had moved there. Well, formerly a friend, anyhow. What if she married, Dottie wondered. Nah, she wasn't the type. Dottie spotted a Ground Round and decided to get a bite to eat. She could look for her acquaintance in the phone book.

After she ordered, she began thinking about Lenny. He'd arrive home, read the note, maybe call Nancy. Who cared? She was free. Free! A rush went through her body, and she clasped her crotch. My gosh, had she orgasmed? That's what this new moment felt like, and there was no way that Lenny, or any thoughts of him would bring her down. She finished her chicken fried steak, side of home fries and even the chocolate malt hit the spot. After using the restroom, she sauntered to the pay phone and swung the attached phone book open to the dense white pages.

Last name, Jeff—oh crap, there were pages of them. And what if she was unlisted?

Sally, no. Sam, nope. There were two Sandras. Could one be her? She inserted a quarter and dialed the first number. A woman answered on the first ring.

228

"Hello?

"Is this Sandy Jeff?"

"Hang on a minute, who's calling, please?"

She almost panicked. "Tell her it's Dot, Dot Campbell. Friend from high school."

"Really? Hi, Dot. I'm Barb, Sandy's roommate."

"Hello, Barb." She accidentally burped. It tasted like chocolate combined with ketchup. "It's nice to meet you."

"Ditto, kiddo. Let me get Sandy. She's gonna be shocked."

Dottie watched a male waiter ogle her from the kitchen. She frowned, and turned away. She suddenly remembered Sandy's speech impediment, how she used to leak her s's out of the corners of her mouth.

"Holy crap, Dottie? Omigod! How are you?"

"Hey, Sandy. Surprise! It's good to hear your voice."

"It's been years. When Barb said it was you, I thought she was joking, like she looked in my yearbook and saw your signature or something. She likes to play practical jokes."

"Oh. Barb, oops, I mean, Sandy." Her stomach was gurgling. "I'm in trouble."

"What kind of trouble?"

She held her tummy. "My husband cheated on me. I drove to

Vegas. I don't know what to do."

"That asshole. I'm sorry, Dot, but I didn't like him before, and now I hate him."

"Yeah, well."

"You're in Vegas? Where?"

"At the Ground Round." She looked through the front glass panels of the restaurant.

"Across from Circus Circus."

"You're less than twenty minutes away from my house. Come over, Dottie. We'll figure out a plan."

"Are you sure, Sandy? I don't want to be a bother."

"Look, what else are you going to do? We've got a spare bed-room, and if you don't mind cats—"

"No, I love animals."

"Yeah, I remember. How about kids?"

"You mean, you got married?"

"Barb's got two. Both girls. Marleen's six and Lexie's three."

"Sounds...nice." Dottie sighed, and realized just how much time had passed since she last saw Sandy.

"Hey, are you still into that God crap? Because that shit will make me crazy if you start."

Dottie smiled, remembering the last time they spoke. "I promise I won't."

"You promise?"

"Uh huh."

Dottie wrote the directions on a napkin. She paid her tab at the Ground Round, crouched above the public toilet to try to rid herself of the gas pains, but to no avail.

Behind the wheel, she slid the Carpenters CD back into play and pushed #6, one of her favorite tracks, "It's Gonna Take Some Time."

Sandy was right. It was only twenty minutes and she found her way easily. She was surprised at the immense houses, and names of the streets, alphabetized names of fruit trees: Apricot Lane, Blossom Road, Cherimoya Court. Was that a fruit? Sandy lived on Hawthorne Avenue, a wide tree-lined street with a median. As she pulled into the driveway, she realized Sandy's speech impediment was gone.

She turned off the car, and got out. Suddenly there was Sandy, running out the front door.

"Holy shit! Dottie!"

"Hey," she said, as Sandy grabbed her in a huge bear hug.

They stood back and looked at each other. Dottie rubbed her eye.

"Where's your stuff?" Sandy asked, peering into the back seat.

"In the trunk."

"Let me get it for you," Sandy said, grabbing her keys.

Dottie retrieved her purse from the passenger floor, as Sandy opened the trunk.

"Girlfriend, you could use new luggage," Sandy said, as Dottie emerged again from the car. And she was right, the beat up TWA suitcase had seen its day.

"Sandy, you look fantastic." She was wearing a yellow Izod shirt, crisply laundered, and short Puma shorts. Her significant tan was stunning and complimented her flaxen, wavy hair, long past her shoulders. When she smiled, it appeared every single tooth was capped, like the model from Crest toothpaste commercials.

"It's part of my work, and thanks, Dottie. You're not so bad yourself."

It was an awkward compliment, adding to Dottie's awful inclination to compare herself to Sandy. She was coming up significantly short.

"Thanks. Sandy. I have to ask—what happened to your...well, your..."

"Speech impediment?" She smiled an even larger, rectangular grin again, displaying her gums. "I worked with a speech therapist for five years, and wore braces for two. Mom and Dad couldn't afford them back in Reno. C'mon, lets get your things in the house. It's nippy out."

Dottie wondered how she'd afforded braces, but was too nervous to ask.

Later that night, Dottie tossed and turned in the guest bedroom. She turned on the reading light for the third time and rubbed her forehead. Was it her fault? Had she pushed Len away? He had changed so much physically since high school. Really let himself go.

And his beer drinking only increased his girth. His hair loss made his forehead endless.

Gradually what little physical intimacy there had been dwindled until he started habitually crashing on the couch, during whatever football or baseball game was in season. They never talked about it; in fact, lying there, Dottie couldn't recall ever having any conversation about sex with Lenny. Not one. She thought about Nancy, wondered where they met, what they talked about. What else did Len get from Nancy that he wasn't getting at home? She felt the panic in her stomach and decided to take a Valium that Barb gave her. She turned the light out and eventually fell into a deep sleep.

"Oh, I thought you were Sandy, you startled me!" Dottie squinted up from the chaise lounge, immediately sun spots covered her vision. She'd dozed off in the backyard. A quick check to make certain her tube top was intact. The heat was sweltering, she licked her parched lips. "And you are?"

"I'm Rick. I live here." He pointed to the white duplex behind him.

Dottie felt self-conscious. Remembered the note that Sandy left on the kitchen table:

'Morning sunshine! Have fun, here's our extra key! Do not let the cat out. Help yourself to the fridge. Call me when you want … 476-2718. Later, Sandy. P.S. Ignore neighbor Rick. He works from home and he's kind of a dick.'

So, this was the dick. And suddenly Dottie wondered what in the world to do. Out there in Sandy's borrowed bikini, a size too small, she felt like skewered barbeque meat.

"I'm Dottie," she offered. Rick held out his hand, Dottie noticed the dirt under his fingernails as she grasped his burly hand.

"I work from home," Rick said. "Nice to meet ya."

He reminded Dottie of a neighbor's golden retriever in Reno, "Happy" was its name.

"Nice to meet you, Rick," Dottie said, trying to conjure a way to bolt back into the house. Had he been watching her?. How long? Her bathing suit bottom felt damp and she slid her towel over her lower half.

"So, you visiting?" Dottie nodded, sipped her iced tea. "You one of them?"

She paused. Did he mean related? She was clueless. "I've known Sandy since we were kids."

"I'm divorced," Rick blurted. "Sandy already knows. My Mormon parents freaked."

"Oh." Again, baffled. "I'm Unitarian." It just came out. She'd used that line for years whenever religion was mentioned. A co-worker had taken the time to explain how liberal Unitarian beliefs are. So, she just couched all of her beliefs in that one phrase.

234

"Uh huh." Rick stepped a few paces back into the shade, closer to the house. "I noticed your ring. You married?"

Dottie shook her head. Thought about her lack of sleep last night. "I was. Well, technically, I am. I mean, on paper."

"Ah, thought maybe you were like them." He nodded toward Sandy's house.

Dottie sipped more iced tea, angling her seat higher. She wondered if her gut hung over her bottoms. Rick fidgeted with his shirt. She wished he'd just go away.

"Like who?"

"Barb and Sandy."

"I haven't the faintest idea, Rick, what you're—"

"They're lezzies. Them kids they have, they're theirs, ya know, as a couple."

Dottie nodded, the shock building adrenaline which coursed through her body. Mixed messages: oh my god, so what, holy shit, who cares, rushed through her mind, as she gained composure. "Rick, I think I have to use the facilities." She stood up. "Will you please excuse me?"

She found the club, Déjà Vu Showgirls, without any problem. Parked in the half full side lot. She'd arrived somewhat early, so she cranked up the air conditioner and listened to the chorus of The Carpenters "Goodbye To Love." Some of the lyrics really struck a nerve: *there may come a time when I may see that I've been wrong, but for now this is my song…I'll say goodbye to love…*

Her first impressions of the club were like being underwater: the dank lighting, the murky cave-like, subterranean theme. Bedrock corridors with flowering plants cascaded, a scent of sweat mingled with lavender and stale alcohol. Her heartbeat increased.

"Can I help you?" A tan man with a stellar smile stood a hair too close. "Are you here for an interview?"

"I'm looking for Sandy Jeff."

"Sandy?" He looked at his watch. Cheshire cat grin. "She's just finishing up. Want to wait in our lounge?"

"Sure." Dottie followed him past a room of exotic women pole dancing to a Gloria Estafan tune, past a bar with a mixture of men and women, and finally into an office-like room—four desks and chairs, a naugahyde couch, and pastel salmon walls.

"You can wait here. Something to drink?"

Dottie said, "No thanks," and sat on the couch.

"She'll be here shortly," the man said, as his walkie talkie garbled a message. She hadn't noticed his shirt said SECURITY until now. "10-4," he replied into the equipment. "I'm on my way."

Once she was alone, Dottie noticed the head shots of dancers hung randomly above the desks: Tamara, Collette, Dixie. She saw the photograph of someone's family vacation, windsurfing, hiking, whitewater kayaking. She wondered if Len ever visited these type of establishments. Sandy burst into the room.

"Been waiting long?"

Dottie shook her head, standing. "Not at all."

"Good, come with me, I want you to meet someone."

Dottie followed her down a lengthy corridor and through vacant rooms that were in disarray. "This place is huge!"

"Yeah."

"You look really tan," Dottie observed.

"Oh, thanks. It's a spray-on," Sandy said.

They'd stopped. The room they were in had three walls. The fourth contained a glass window with a mini-set of bleachers inside the glass box. "This is the kind of room I work." Dottie nodded. "Paying customers come here, where we're standing. They can see me—but I can't see them under the stage lights. Best of all, they can't touch me because of the glass."

Dottie nodded, thinking this is one of the most bizarre things she'd experienced. "And what do you do in there?"

Sandy smiled. "Depends upon the day. Use your imagination, Dottie."

Dottie was not certain that she wanted to. "Wow, must be exhausting."

"It can be. C'mon, follow me."

Finally Sandy led her to a u-shaped booth with a glass table. A Hispanic-looking waitress in a skimpy outfit approached.

"Want something? Oh, hey Sandy."

"Marisol, this is Dottie. We'll have two Water Moccasins."

"Coming right up!"

Dottie felt like she was in some boat, going down a river filled with rapids. Thrill of what she was unclear. But a cavalier feeling had replaced some of her fear.

"I met your neighbor."

"Rick the dick? You poor thing," Sandy sighed.

"He wasn't so bad."

"Did he come to our door?"

"No, I was sunning in the backyard. I fell asleep and the next thing I knew—"

"That pig, Dottie. I hope you ignored him." Marisol delivered the drinks and flounced off.

"I tried to." They chuckled, sipped their drinks. "Mmm, tastes good, like a popsicle."

"I know, careful—they can be lethal."

"He mentioned something about you. And Barb."

"Oh?" Sandy raised one eyebrow. A man approached the table. She slid closer to Dottie. "Rocco, meet Dottie!" She patted her spot where she'd been sitting.

"Hello." Dottie noticed his height, well over six feet, and the immensity of his shoulders. She held out her hand. "Nice to meet you."

"My pleasure." Rocco smiled, taking her hand. Dottie's hand felt diminutive in his and she suppressed a giggle. He was very handsome, like a young Burt Reynolds.

"I told Rocco what happened, Dottie."

"I'm so sorry, Ma'am," he said.

"I'm not sure I understand," Dottie said.

Sandy exchanged a quick glance with Rocco, then looked around the room. In a lowered voice she said, "Dottie, we'd like to offer you a possible retaliation. You can't let that bastard get away with what he did to you."

Suddenly it dawned on her what Sandy was saying. "But Sandy, even if I, I don't have any money to—"

"Rocco owes me one," she said, and Rocco nodded, with a lopsided grin.

Dottie pondered the possibilities. What were they talking about exactly? She took another sip of her drink. Sandy crossed her arms. "I can't. I'm sorry, Sandy. I just — I can't."

"Rocco, take a hike, give us five." He got up and walked away. Sandy took a deep breath, then stared into Dottie's eyes. "I have a secret, Dottie. Something that I have never told you because I was afraid it would hurt you more than it did me."

Dottie sat back against the bancard, trying to steal herself against whatever Sandy was about to tell her. "Okay, go on."

239

"Our senior trip to Mount Rushmore. We were roommates, and Len's room was adjacent. His roommate was Walter Whitmore." She stopped to take a long slug of her drink. "We went to that karaoke bar, remember? The one with the marquee that had the same presidents' heads made out of plastic?"

Slowly the memories came back. "Yes," Dottie nodded.

"I felt sick from all that beer, we were sneaking it from some guy's truck. I think I made myself throw up before I decided to walk back to the hotel. You asked Len to make sure I got back to our hotel safely. And last minute, Walter joined us."

"I wasn't with you, too?"

Sandy shook her head. "No, you wanted to stay because your turn hadn't come up to sing." She paused for some time. "When we got back to the hotel, I thought the guys would just get me to my room. I'd brush my teeth, hit the sack, hopefully the room wouldn't be spinning too hard." Sandy's face looked grim. "Unfortunately, it didn't go down that way." She paused and took a sip of her drink.

Dottie swallowed hard, tried to look away, couldn't. She wanted to close her eyes, sink into in her cozy recliner back home, kick back to a Carpenters classic. Instead she felt shaky. "Go on."

"I'll spare you the gory details. Suffice it to say that I was a virgin up until that night. And Len, who I'd respected; well, he initiated it."

"Initiated?" Dottie shrugged.

"You really are—" Sandy scratched her arm. "Guess I have to spell it out. Len raped me, and for the next hour or so, seemed

240

like days, they took turns. He, then Walter."

Dottie felt her mouth drop open. Recalled a conversation she and Len had just before they got married when they'd revealed facts about their virginal status with his family priest. "I don't know what to say."

Sandy paused. "Yeah, neither did I. And I blamed myself. I trusted them, and they took advantage. Simple as that. I was stupid and I paid the price." She scrunched her mouth into a tight line. "But, never again." Just as she finished, Rocco approached the table and sat again at the booth.

Dottie crossed her legs, considering what Sandy just told her. "So, what are we talking about here?"

"You need more time?" Rocco asked Sandy.

"No!" Sandy put her hand on Rocco's. "Stay." She turned to Dottie. "Rocco has…connections. All you need to do is say, 'okay,' or 'just do it,' and we're all over it."

"Okay, but before I do that, what are my options?"

Sandy nodded at Rocco, smiling.

"Well, we could do any version of what we call Nuts & Bolts," he said. "Basically he's gonna spend a few days in the hospital, and will more than likely not reproduce."

Dottie winced. "What else?" She tried to imagine just how the Nuts & Bolts would be carried out.

"Oh, there's an entire menu of options." Sandy exchanged glances with Rocco, nodded at him, grinned at Dottie. "Let's go back to my house. I'll ride with you, and we'll follow Rocco.

Sound good?"

"Sure," Dottie said. "Can I use a bathroom first?"

When they arrived at the house, Barb's silver Audi was parked in the driveway.

Dottie turned off the Taurus, and put her hand on Sandy's arm. "Wait," she said. "I just want to ask you one thing."

Sandy turned to face her, motioning a delay to Rocco who had already gotten out of her car. "What's up?"

"Are you and Barb a couple?"

Sandy looked away. "No."

"Then why'd your neighbor tell me that you are?"

"We're just roommates. Barb told Rick that we were lesbians because she slept with him right after his wife moved out. She was drunk, and he took it as the second coming or something. Anyhow, before I knew it she'd used us as her "out.""

"So, you don't like women then?"

"I never said that." Sandy smiled. "I just said Barb isn't my girlfriend."

Dottie wasn't sure if she was glad she brought it up or not.

Barb greeted them at the door, and Dottie noticed it seemed as though she and Rocco had met before. "Let's sit in here," Barb said, motioning to the living room. There were already drinks set on a TV stand. "Anyone want a glass of lemonade? It's homemade, not that mixed crap."

"I'll take one," Dottie said. "I'm parched."

"It's the Vegas air," Sandy said. "So dry." She was holding a tray out to Dottie.

"Snickerdoodle?"

Dottie took one, passed them to Rocco.

Barb handed her a glass of lemonade. "So, Dottie, Sandy told me all about your... situation." She sat on the black leather sofa next to Dottie. "First of all, let me say, I'm really, really sorry."

"Yeah, well," Dottie said. She sipped her drink. It needed more sugar.

Sandy scoffed, "Sorry, my ass."

"Sandy, please," Barb said. She turned to Dottie. "I want to apologize in advance."

"Apologize... for Len being a creep?"

"Yes, that and also that I have to show you these photos." She turned to pick up her briefcase.

"Photos?" Dottie said. "What photos?"

Barb clicked open the latches on her briefcase and pulled out a manila envelope. She undid the fastener and took out a stack of 8x10 photographs. "These photos," she said, handing the first one to Dottie. "Is that your husband?"

Dottie nodded. "Where'd you get this?"

"I'm a PI," Barb replied.

Dottie looked at the photo again, Len in bed with a woman she'd never seen, labeled 'Nadine.' "PI?"

"Barb's a private investigator. Before that she was Special Crimes Unit of a government office," Sandy said.

"What government office?" Dottie asked.

"I can't tell you more or I'd have to kill you," Barb joked.

They all laughed, except Dottie. "Show me all of them," she said, indicating the stack of photos in Barb's lap. As she leafed through every single one, slowly, an anesthesia spread through her veins. The room fell away, the only sound registering was the tick-tock, tick-tock of the grandfather clock in the adjacent hallway. An image of an unending body of water rolled up, and she saw herself walking further and further into the deep as the waves lapped higher: her waist, her chest, her neck... She imagined the Carpenters Greatest Hits playing on a looped track.

"Dottie?" Sandy's voice brought her back to the room.

There was a long pause. She felt all eyes on her. "Kill him."

Simo Freeshow

I was sipping a Dos Equis at Life Café. It was summer, and the heat radiated from the sidewalks. Even so, I enjoyed the patio, watching mothers push strollers into Tompkins Square Park, skateboarders blur by, squirrels foraging in the oaks that lined 10th Street. My androgynous waiter delivered my nachos.

"A nice spicy dish on a hot day," he said, a British accent.

"It's addictive."

"I'm Seymour," he said. He tucked a long, thick strand of hair behind his ear.

"Evan," I said. "I've seen you before." The café was one of my watering holes. I was a hair and makeup artist. I popped into Life Café because it was close to Stuyvesant Town. My best pal, Trudy, offered her place when I was booted from my sub-let. Trudy already had a roommate, so I temporarily crashed on her foldout living room couch.

Turns out he was English. Seymour lived way west on 14th street. He told me his last name was Freeshow, and I couldn't stop laughing.

"Don't you get it?" I finally said.

"It's not that funny. It's my name."

That was the first time we kissed. We were walking his two humungous mastiffs that weekend. Folks parted like the Red Sea. We stopped at the mighty Hudson, churning a rubbish gray. Jersey loomed, a mirage of buildings, beige breathing outlines.

I looked at Seymour. He wore a pale blue tank, and camouflage shorts. He smelled of peaches and bicycle grease. His physical beauty burst from every pore. It felt time slowed down, like I'd never seen him before.

He turned to me, like a long movie close-up. Who cares who kissed who first, but there were fireworks. Right there on the West Side Highway. No one gave a rat's ass except us: one of the things I love about New York. Okay, his dogs were a little jealous.

The next weekend, Seymour (now "Simo," as his English mates called him) and I drove upstate to Woodstock. We hiked in the mountains. I took him to Omega Institute near charming Rhinebeck. We shared a hammock, snuggling and exploring, then napped. We ate a delicious vegetarian dinner. That night, returning back to Manhattan, I asked him to stay overnight. He said "yes" before I'd finished.

It's always odd to sleep with a new boyfriend. I'm not a great sleeper. But add to that mix Trudy's foldout couch, and her roommate, plus Trudy's two cats that became a little nutty around 4 a.m.

There was lots of tossing, turning. Finally, by the first glimmers of sunrise, I was dreaming. But no, Simo was going to town under the sheets. Waves of pleasure rolled through me. I grabbed my pillow to muffle my moans and closed my eyes. I was so ecstatic, I almost didn't hear Trudy shuffle past on her way to the kitchen. My mouth dropped open as I pulled away from Simo. We were busted.

"Wish it were me," Trudy said.

The Empty Nest

The kitchen was silent with the exception of my slurps. I was still slunk down in the corner, downing that last bit of Ben & Jerry's Chunky Monkey, the freezing cold oozing bits sliding down my throat. I wanted to stop, wanted to throw the carton against the stove backsplash. Wanted to scream, "Why'd you leave?" when I knew the reasons. I heard Megan plodding down the stairs. I jumped up. Opened the nearest cupboard filled with spices and tossed the nearly empty quart in there. Pretended I was finishing the dishes.

"What're you still doing up?" Megan asked. She reached for a glass, and filled it from the fridge.

"Can't sleep," I said. "Wanna help finish the tree?"

Megan had recently bleached her hair. Wasn't the first time. But now she'd streaked magenta through the entire maze. "Yer gonna ruin your hair," I'd warned.

"Big deal. It's my hair," was her reply.

I wanted to say, "But I'm the one who has to look at it!" Instead I just nodded.

"The tree?" she asked. "Are we still gonna go through the façade, Mom?"

The hot water scalded my hands. It felt good, but I turned it off. Grabbed a dishtowel.

"It's not a façade, Megan. It's a holiday about Jesus. After all, he died for our sins."

She snorted. "Yeah. Thanks for the reminder. And I nearly died just thinking about it all these years." She yawned.

I thought about her cutting herself. The reason I'd started going to church. Alone. He wasn't interested. Thought I was overreacting. I needed something to hold onto. Belief in something larger than myself when I couldn't fathom why Megan would do something so brutal to her own flesh.

"Nah, I'll pass on the tree." Dragged her heavy feet back toward the stairs. "G'night."

My youngest half-sister, Nicole, dropped by the next day. She liked to appear out of nowhere, like a cyclone. No call or text in advance, no warning.

"I was on my way to the cleaners and wanted to bring you this," she said. Handed me an envelope with just my name, Jodi, scribbled on it. I knew it was from Dad before I saw the writing.

Nicole took her new Uggs off. "Aren't you going to open it?" she asked. She sat at the family room table.

"Nah, I'll read it later." I hadn't talked to Dad since Marv had moved out. They worked together in the same law office.

"You should see how Lindsay just devours those Laura Ingalls Wilder books you gave me."

"Oh really?" I set her coffee in front of her, and went back to add more milk and sugar to mine.

"I have to make her stop long enough to get her to do her math and science projects."

Nicole was homeschooling her kids; Lindsay was the eldest of her three darlings.

"Well, I'm happy she likes them so much. I remember enjoying them when I was younger, too."

"Your tree looks nice," Nicole nodded toward the half assembled plastic bush.

"We're not finished yet."

"Oh. How's Megan?" She sipped her coffee.

"Fine." I didn't have any reason not to trust her. Just didn't.

"How's she handling the whole Marv moving out thing?"

I shrugged. "I guess, okay. We don't really talk about it much."

Nicole stared then her cell rang. "Sorry," she said, glancing at the number. "I've gotta get this." She stood up and walked to the window as if I wouldn't be able to hear her. "Honey? What is it? I'm over at Aunt Jodi's. You're supposed to play nice together. Don't make me call Daddy. Okay? Mommy loves you. Bye." Turned to me. "Sorry. I guess our new tutor sucks."

New tutor? What happened to the last three? "So, any plans for Christmas?"

Her eyes lit up. "Well, we're going over to Grandpa and Grandma's after we open our gifts. You know, this is probably going to be Sybille's last year believing in Santa Claus."

Sybille was seven.

"I don't think Megan ever believed in Santa Claus."

"I heard that." I turned to see Megan rubbing her eyes and yawning at the kitchen sink. "More snow?" she groaned, looking out the window.

Nicole jumped up. "Hello, Megan." She walked over to her. "Can I have a hug?"

Megan hugged her, while mugging a face toward me.

"I like your hair," Nicole said. "It's—unusual." She smiled.

Megan poured a mug of coffee. "How can you be so perky this early?"

"I've been up since 5!"

"That's about the time I fell asleep." They laughed.

We all settled at the table. Megan's hair stuck out in about a thousand directions. I wanted to smooth it, to lacquer it. To buzz it off and start over.

"I have an idea," Nicole was saying. "We're going to Costa Rica in January."

"Lucky you," Megan said. "I hear they grow good weed." Nicole laughed.

"Megan!" I warned.

"Just kidding, Mom, chill."

"What I wondered," Nicole continued, "is when you start

school, Megan?"

She shrugged, and looked at me. "Any idea, Mom?"

"I think it's the 14th? I'd have to check the calendar."

Nicole smiled. "How would you like to come with us, Megan? As our nanny?"

I suppressed a laugh. Megan nudged me under the table.

There was a long pause. "I don't speak Spanish," she said.

Nicole giggled. "They all speak English, or some form of it."

"I think they call it pigeon?" I said.

"No, Mom, that's—"

"Oh my god, look at the time!" Nicole said. She jumped up. "I forgot, it's Saturday. Garrison has his private swim lesson. And, I just have to tell you… All the kids begin lessons in Minnow. Well, in three lessons, Garrison was already a Shark! He jumped, like, six levels. He's such an amazing kid." She downed the rest of her coffee. "I'll e-mail you the dates of our trip and some pictures of the resort. Megan, we'll have a blast!"

I followed her to the door, and watched while she pulled her boots on. "Say hello to everyone." I knew it was lame, being so vague, but it was the best I could do.

"Merry Christmas, Jodi," she whispered in my ear.

...
Notes
...

Section 1: I'd like to thank the editors of the following magazines in which some of these pieces originally appeared:

Metazen, Negative Suck, Thunderclap, amphibi.us, Postcard Shorts, Elimae, The Airgonaut, Stripped (print anthology), Short, Fast and Deadly, HOUSEFIRE, Jumping Blue Gods, Birdville Magazine, Thrice Fiction, Whistling Fire, Levure Litteraire, States of Terror (print anthology).

Section 2: The idea for this project was steeped in my love for Edward Gorey's The Gashleycrumb Tinies. Huge thanks to Bob Schofield for his amazing artistic interpretation of the kids in this imaginary classroom. "Aretha" appeared in Literary Orphans.

Section 3: This collaboration began with the wizardry of Joseph Quintela when he created the Word Poeticizer. He asked the following poets/writers to re-define the English language, word by word: Liz Axelrod, Tyron Bailey, Craig Cady, Gabriel Don, Joseph Don, Apparently Joseph, mcsherry, Alissa Morhordt- Goldstein, Maggie, Michael O'Brien, Jennifer- Leigh Prihory, Joseph A.W. Quintela, Joseph Schroeder, Jeremiah Thimpson, David Tomaloff, Leah Umansky, Eryk Wenziak, and myself.

I then fed a lyric from each female songstress into the Word Poeticizer, and out popped an entirely new prose poem. After several edits, I asked Eryk Wenziak to re-design each individual prose poem on the page.

Section 4: I'd like to thank the editors of the following magazines in which some of these pieces originally appeared:

Elimae, Drunk Monkeys, Gay Flash Fiction, The Not, In Those Days We (print), Other Room, Scabies anthology (forthcoming).

Bob Schofield is the author and illustrator of The Inevitable June, Moon Facts, and Man Bites Cloud. He lives in Rotterdam. He likes what words and pictures do. He wants to be a ghostly presence in your life. You can find him here: bobschofield.tumblr.com, and on Twitter @anothertower.

Joseph A. W. Quintela creates art that explores themes of natural affinities, material excess, and a curious interplay between the exuberant and the meditative. His practice harnesses a fluency in a variety of media including paint, LED light, books, and culinary ingredients. Solo exhibitions in New York have included Between Two Worlds (2016), The Quarters Project (2015), Portrait of the Cast of You in Eye (2013) and FOOT | KNOTS (2012). Ongoing displays of his work are installed at The Strand, Central Booking (LES), and Salinas Restaurant (Chelsea). He is the founding editor of Deadly Chaps Press and created the Working Definitions project in 2012 with programmer, Noah Jacobson.
www.josephquintela.com

Joseph A. W. Quintela
Web | Facebook | Instagram

Eryk Wenziak is art director of A-minor Press, art editor of A-minor magazine, and Editor-in-Chief of rigormort. us. His poetry has been published in numerous journals and anthologies and his photography and artwork have been featured in several gallery exhibitions around the Brooklyn and NYC area. He is the author of four chapbooks, has been nominated for two Pushcart Prizes, and has a full-length book of visual poetry and collage titled "i need space," being published in the spring of 2017 by Deadly Chaps Press, followed by a gallery exhibition and book release where prints from the book will be on display. As a designer, Eryk's photography has been used as the cover of six full-length collections of poetry by well-known authors. His artwork is currently represented and sold by the Brooklyn-based Smith and Jones Gallery and various limited-edition prints and original pieces of his work are also available for sale on his personal website.

www.erykwenziak.com
www.smithandjonesart.com/eryk-wenziak/

Robert Vaughan leads roundtables at Red Oak Writing in Milwaukee, WI. He also teaches workshops in hybrid writing, dialogue, playwriting at places like The Clearing in Door County, WI.

He was the co-founder of Flash Fiction Fridays, a radio program on WUWM in Milwaukee, where he premiered local flash fiction writers, and also starred writers from America and abroad.

He is a senior editor for JMWW, and Lost in Thought magazines, a guest editor for Uno Kudo #5. He is also the an editor at (b)OINK. His books are *Microtones; Addicts & Basements; Diptrychs, Dipshits and Lipsticks*; as well as *Rift*, co-authored with Kathy Fish, is his fourth collection.

His writing has been published in over 500 various literary journals, such as Necessary Fiction, Elimae,

Literary Orphans, Everyday Genius, The Lit Pub, and Nervous Breakdown.

He's also been selected for many anthologies such as Stripped (2012), Flash Fiction Funny (2014), and This is Poetry (2015).

He is the author of three collections: *Microtones* (Cervena Barva Press, 2012); *Diptychs + Triptychs + Lipsticks + Dipshits* (Deadly Chaps, 2013); and *Addicts & Basements* (CCM, 2014). He is also the co-author of *Rift* (Unknown Press, 2015*)*, a split book of flash fiction written with Kathy Fish.

He also edited Flash Fiction Fridays (2011). His awards include Micro-Fiction (2012), Gertrude Stein Awards (2013, 2014) and a Professional of the Year Award from Strathmore's Who's Who for outstanding contributions and achievements as an author (2015).

Made in the USA
San Bernardino, CA
08 February 2017